Hungry Hungry Hoodoo

Liz Schulte

-Missouri-

Printed in the United States of America

Copyright © 2013 by Liz Schulte
Formatting by JT Formatting

ISBN-13: 978-1482784374
ISBN-10: 1482784378

All rights reserved.

Without limiting the rights under copyright reserved above, no part of this publication may be reproduced, stored in or introduced into a retrieval system, or transmitted, in any form, or by any means (electronic, mechanical, photocopying, recording, or otherwise) without the prior written permission of the author of this book.

This is a work of fiction. Names, characters, places, brands, media, and incidents are either the product of the author's imagination or are used fictitiously. The author acknowledges the trademarked status and trademark owners of various products referenced in this work of fiction, which have been used without permission. The publication/use of these trademarks is not authorized, associated with, or sponsored by the trademark owners.

Praise for Liz Schulte's Secrets

Olivia and Holden are the couple that you love to see fight and make up. The fire between the two of them makes the book a page turner alone. Throw in the obstacles (I don't want to give anything away!) that they're up against, and the book consumes you. I CANNOT wait to see what Choices (Book #2) brings for our beloved couple, and to find out what their fates will hold.

This book is a page turner. The story is vivid and the characters and story are brought to life off the page.

This was an emotional and mysterious story that got me hooked early on and as the story progressed it just got better and better. I felt like it was different from other paranormal books I've read but in a positive sense.

Schulte did a fab job of keeping the story moving, I fell completely in love/lust? with Holden (who wouldn't?) and Olivia is a strong female character who I think women can relate to -- so much coming at her that's confusing and scary, yet she seems to figure out much of it and still stay strong...eventually.

The ending -- oooh, Liz. You leave us wanting so much more. The mark of an excellent author.

I immediately fell in love with the characters in this book. The author does an amazing job of making the reader empathize and even root for the most terrible people.

Liz Schulte is quickly becoming my favorite author. She will soon be sharing shelf space with Anne Rice and Kim Harrison and I have very limited shelf space. Forget Twilight, forget the Hunger Games; this is the new series to follow and fall in love with.

This was one of those books that I couldn't put down and read deep into the night. We get to hear both Liv's and Holden's versions of what is going on and OH HOLDEN! Ultimate bad boy but he has incredible depth to him.

For my third floor girls

ONE

I stood in my scorched, hollowed-out yoga studio, turning in a listless circle, too numb to feel. The storefront was a wet, smoldering pile of ash and the building, merely a shell.

"Was anyone hurt?" I asked, barely recognizing my own voice. Numb was too small of a word—shell-shocked was more accurate.

"No." Femi's voice came from the doorway. I didn't even know she was there. She prowled around the room, silent as death, her green cat eyes collecting every detail. "It happened overnight."

I took a shaky breath. "That's good."

"Officially this is an electrical fire," Cheney said, and Sy snorted. I looked back at the guys, but mostly at Cheney. Just looking at him made my knees a little weak.

"Why would anyone want to burn down your studio?" Sy asked. "It's just so …"

Evil, hurtful, devastating—

"Bold," Femi supplied.

I nodded and kicked a piece of sodden, smoking wood.

I hadn't been back here in months, but losing my studio this way felt like seeing a part of myself destroyed.

"Was it rebels?" I whispered with equal parts suspicion and surprise. I hadn't figured out my relationship with the rebels, but maybe they were as hostile toward me as Cheney believed. "Or the elves?" That made more sense . . . They really hated me. Most of them refused to acknowledge me, even though I was their queen consort or whatever.

Not for the first time, I wondered if the cost of Cheney and me being together was an unfair one for him to pay. It seemed he had one fire to put out after another because of us—because of *me*.

I glanced at Cheney. With his wild hair, gleaming golden eyes, and sharp-tipped ears, he looked grim and breathtaking in the scorched, dark space. He no longer used his glamour—had chosen not to disguise his elfin features with human ones—ever since he forcibly took the crown from his father and became Erlking. It was something else I was going to have to get used to—much like this constant pull in my chest toward him.

"Rebels," Cheney said with an air of finality.

Sy lifted his golden eyebrows, and I bit my lip and turned away from them. I didn't know what to think anymore. On one hand I had my cousin, Sy, who I was beginning to think I didn't know nearly enough about. He seemed to know a little about everything happening in the Abyss. Sy was connected, no doubt, but was he impartial? Even though we were related, I didn't feel a familial connection, so it was hard to imagine he was only involved to help me. Not being able to remember my life as one of them, and being told that I'd chosen to come to earth as a human rather than recalling that information myself, had been infuriating before—and was driving me insane now.

Sy wanted me to come and stay with him until my memory returned and I figured out which side I should fall on. He thought the fact that I'd apparently had some sort of relationship with Jaron, the rebel leader, meant I needed to distance myself from Cheney. And it probably was the prudent thing to do, but I refused.

Then there was Cheney, the Erlking and my magically bound husband. He definitely wasn't impartial, but from what I had seen and learned about him since he walked back into my life, he was a good man. The trouble was I couldn't bring myself to fully trust my feelings for him. I'd dabbled in magic long enough to know that spells having to do with the heart were tricky. Done right they could make a person with no feelings for another person suddenly be madly in love. Having a husband was scary enough; having a magically bound husband who I never had a chance to choose kept me on edge most of the time.

I was walking a thin line, and a strong wind in any direction could tip me. If I chose to explore my rebel connections, I could lose Cheney—and he'd waited so long to get me back, I didn't know how much more he would take. But ignoring the connection might mean I was turning my back on what I believed.

I lifted my hand and touched Cheney's smooth, lovely face. Real or not, right now I loved him.

And maybe I didn't have a decision looming over me. Maybe I was exactly where I was supposed to be, so why ruin everything by overthinking? That's what I wanted to believe, anyway, but a nagging feeling said I could be wrong —stupid elf side.

Cheney wrapped an arm around my waist, and I almost sighed with relief as I leaned my head against his shoulder. Magical bonds are not to be taken lightly. The magnetic pull of them was painful when denied. When we weren't touching, I felt his absence—a dull, constant ache in my center. If the need wasn't fulfilled, it grew.

Cheney endured years of agony while we were separated, while I was living a human life and felt nothing. Now that my elf side was back in full force, I could hardly make it half a day without wanting to curl up and cry if he wasn't at my side. I leaned my head against his shoulder and closed my eyes to the ashes of my past that surrounded me. I had planned on never coming back anyway, right? So this didn't matter. Not really. Maybe losing the studio—my last physical connection to my fully human side—was for the best. I had to find a way to be content in my new life. It was where I belonged now. I struggled with a lump in my throat.

"So why did you call us here?" Cheney asked Femi, and I frowned. Wasn't the destruction of my studio reason enough?

Femi waved us to the back and nudged my office door open with her foot. A knife stuck out of the center of my blackened desk. I pulled away from Cheney to get a closer look. A picture of Michael was tacked to the top of the desk with the knife.

"Do you know who this is?" Femi asked.

"My ex-fiancé. Michael," I breathed. I pulled out my cell phone and dialed Michael's number. It went directly to voice mail. I looked back at them.

"He's a human?" Sy asked. I nodded. "What's his last name?"

"Christian."

Sy pulled out his own phone and walked away.

"Is this a threat?" I looked between Femi and Cheney. "We have to find him. Warn him."

Cheney scowled. "No, we need to slow down and think things through. How are you going to warn him when you can't tell him about our world? What if he's already dead?" He crossed his arms over his chest. "What we need is to have your coven and your grandmother move back into the castle until we can be sure they're safe. What we *don't* need is to panic and involve humans."

"They can't just drop everything. They have lives."

"Exactly, and I'm protecting those lives. They're an asset to our kingdom."

I sputtered, not knowing what to say. My friends were not *assets*. They were practically my family. I didn't appreciate him viewing them in such a cold manner.

"Cheney's right, Selene. Don't panic. We'll figure everything out," Femi said. "Wait and see what Sy's up to."

I called each of the girls, who all agreed a little too willingly to come back—I guess no one likes their day job—and let Cheney call my grandmother while we waited for Sy to return. Finally he reappeared in the doorway, his hands stuffed in the pockets of his worn jeans—a pose that made his biceps bulge the sleeves of his faded black Batman shirt. As ever when I studied him, I looked for a family resemblance—and found none. Similar golden, tan skin and slightly pointed ears, but that was it. His hair was as blond as mine was dark, and his eyes were so silver they were almost mirrored. Mine had been described as pools of honey. My inability to see or feel our blood connection aside, however, I liked Sy a lot. He was open, friendly, and, best of all, he never compared me to the way I used to be.

"Michael was reported missing this morning." Sy's eyes locked on me. "You want me to start looking into this?"

I nodded and Cheney said, "If you have time, great. Unfortunately, Selene and I have too much to do to allow the rebels to divert our attention. I hope the human is alive."

"Right, you wouldn't want to waste your time *saving* someone's life," Femi said.

Cheney never talked about elf business outside of the castle. Sebastian, Cheney, and I were trying to sift through mounds of records to figure out what his father had been up to. I wasn't sure I was useful, since I couldn't read ninety percent of the documents because they were in a foreign language, but Cheney liked for me to be there. We were also making plans to invite all the fae races to choose a representative to serve on his council. I had only seen my friends a handful of times—at the coven meetings, to be more precise—since we took over. Being a queen wasn't all it was cracked up to be. However, I wasn't about to let office duties stand in the way of protecting those I loved. Michael and I hadn't worked out, but I still cared about him, and he was in danger because of me.

Cheney glared at Femi. "It isn't like that. I want to save the human too, but we have obligations and can't afford to lose any more time."

I closed my eyes, doubting Cheney's statement. He didn't like Michael; he couldn't even say his name. I didn't think he cared a whit whether he lived or died. I didn't blame him, exactly, but it didn't change how I felt either. "I can't ignore something like this," I said. "You and Sebastian can carry on without me. I have to help Sy and Femi."

"Mmm, no. That's not a good idea." Cheney shook his head. "Whoever did this was probably hoping for this response. You're playing into their hands."

"If no one else will say it, I will," Femi purred, one hand on her jutted hip, her bronze skin rippling with emotion. "This sure as hell wasn't an electrical fire, and I'd be willing to bet a life that the so-called rebels didn't do this either. The human might still be alive. You can't just ignore that."

Femi's goddess heritage was showing in full force, and as she stared down Cheney, her vertical pupils almost disappeared. I took a step back.

Unlike me, however, Cheney didn't seem the least bit intimidated by her take-no-shit-from-anyone attitude or the fighting stance her leather-clad, cat-lithe muscular body had suddenly assumed.

"Relax, Sekhmet. We'll figure something out," Cheney grumbled.

Her posture eased and she winked at me when I stared too long, snapping me back to reality. "Sorry. So what do we do?"

She laughed. "That's what I like about you. You haven't had a clue what's going on since I met you, but you're always in the thick of it. What other enemies do you have, Hermione?"

"Human Selene," I patted myself on the chest, "doesn't have enemies. But the half-elf me was apparently a bitch that no one liked." I ran my hands through my hair. "You guys know more about who hated me most than I do." I couldn't wrap my mind around why Jaron and his men would destroy my studio. It wasn't a logical move if they wanted me to come back.

Femi gave me a peculiar look before spinning around and walking away with her phone in hand. I moved in the opposite direction, needing to be in motion.

"I like you, coz." Sy gave me a lop-sided grin. My eyes filled with tears and his eyes widened slightly. "We'll find this guy. Don't worry."

"I wish I remembered something. Anything. Why can't people leave me alone?"

No one could explain why awakening my elf half hadn't brought back my memories. My grandmother, Edith Meriweather, and my coven had cast every spell they could think of the past weeks, trying to recover my memory—with pathetic results. Each memory they managed to return came with pain. It started off small with headaches but intensified with every new spell. Now, sensations ranged from feeling I was eating broken glass to being hit with a bat. On occasion there had even been blood. And nothing I remembered seemed significant in any way or helped me understand anything better.

I was everyone's favorite topic of discussion. What's wrong with Selene? She's not *herself*. My human friends insisted I'd changed, always pointing out the elf. Cheney and his second in command, Sebastian, always pointed out my human weaknesses. I had begun to spend a lot more time alone because they all got on my nerves.

"You will get your memories back. Just be patient," Cheney said.

"We don't have time for patience—and how do you know I will? What if I don't and someone takes Grandma or my friends or you?" I threw my arms up in the air. "I can't keep dealing with all the things I did wrong in the past. It's driving me crazy. I can't put everyone else in danger because I seemed to have made one bad decision after another." By the end of my rant I was shouting and the already unstable room was vibrating. I needed to calm down. I took a deep breath and shut down the fear, worry, and panic threatening to take over.

Femi slung her arm over my shoulder. "We'll get to the bottom of this, but there's nothing we can do tonight. You need a night out away from everything." She led me toward the door, ignoring Cheney's and my objections. "Don't wait up, boys."

Femi dragged me out of the studio and to her car. We needed to look for Michael, but nevertheless, here we were, walking into a weird bar one scary-fast car ride later. The place was called Snow, and everything inside was stark white except for the black lights that made the room glow. I followed Femi to a table where Olivia, a guardian, sat with an amused expression.

"You managed to get away from your guard dog?" Femi asked, quirking an eyebrow.

Olivia shook her head. "If Holden knew I intended to meet you at yet *another* jinn bar, I would've never made it out of the house." She laughed, not looking overly upset.

I glanced around the room again, wondering what she meant by a "jinn bar." From Sebastian's lessons I knew jinn were supposed to be bad, but if that was true, what were we doing there?

"Damn, I always forget," Femi said, taking a chair to the left of Olivia.

I sat too. "It's not safe here?"

Olivia laughed. "Not at all. Femi's idea of a girls' night out isn't the same as yours or mine. She likes to poke bears."

Femi held up her hands innocently. "I just want to have a good time. We're perfectly safe. Olivia is the scariest person in here." Olivia laughed again and shrugged. I doubted she could frighten anyone. "But enough talk. Let's dance." Femi was on the dance floor in a flash, her body becoming one with the music. I looked at Olivia and she got up, her blue-green eyes twinkling.

"Stay near me," she said in my ear.

I nodded. As soon as I stepped down the two steps and onto the dance floor, my mind was wiped clear. I didn't think or feel anything except the vibrating beat. A hand brushed my arm and instinctively I followed the touch, my mind blank.

"No, you don't," Olivia said behind me, catching my shoulder and keeping her hand there. Everything cleared. The ache from being away from Cheney was back, along with worry and uncertainty—I liked the dreamy haze better. Olivia held onto me until I turned back to her and Femi. "We shouldn't have come here, Femi," Olivia shouted over the music.

"Why?" Femi yelled back. Olivia nodded in my direction, and I suddenly felt like a child who couldn't take care of herself and I didn't like it. I was perfectly capable. "She's fine," Femi said. "You're a fighter, aren't you, Selene?"

Damn right, my inner voice said. *I could make all these people my puppets if I wanted.* The thought made me smile and feel a little better. The muscles in my shoulders loosened as we danced and laughed with each other. After several songs, another hand brushed my elbow, but it wasn't the same this time. The sensation was familiar, but not alluring. I turned around and Jaron was behind me. My stomach dropped and I was flooded with curiosity and trepidation. I backed up, plowing directly into Femi.

He held his hands up in a surrendering gesture, though his eyes sparked with something else. "I just want to talk."

"Get out of here, Jaron." Femi came around me. "Selene's taking the night off."

I hadn't been able to get away from the castle long enough, or alone, to talk to Jaron—and I needed to hear what he had to say, whether I wanted to or not. I had to know what happened before I became a changeling, and obviously Cheney's information was one sided. Jaron could fill in a lot of missing gaps.

I took a deep breath and stepped around Femi. "It's okay." I looked up at Jaron. He was so tall and broad, I felt tiny. "Let's talk."

Femi's stare drilled into my back as I walked off the dance floor and to our table. The fact that Jaron made her nervous made me nervous. I sat in Olivia's chair and nodded to the seat across from me. "How did you find me?"

"I followed you."

"Where's Michael?"

"Who's Michael?" he asked, his heavy eyebrows pulling together. I glared, and his lips tilted up slightly. "Yet another lover, Selene? My, my, you have been busy." His voice was cold and harsh.

The ever-so-brief memory I had the first time I met Jaron crept into my mind and made me look down. He was definitely my boyfriend at some point, but I didn't know when or why we broke up. "What do you want from me?" Was I asking him or the part of myself that urged me to go with Jaron and forget about Michael and Cheney? *Oh, multiple personalities, thy name is Selene.*

He rubbed his rough jaw line. "At the moment? An explanation will do."

An explanation? Didn't we all want that? What the hell was elf Selene thinking? The club was too noisy to have a conversation like this. I wasn't going to shout about what a lunatic I was or that I was possibly stringing along two men. "We can't talk here."

His jaw stiffened and his cloud-gray eyes iced over. He offered his hand. "I'll take you anywhere you want to go."

I shook my head. "I'll arrange a time through Sy to meet with you. Don't follow me again."

Jaron's shoulders straightened and those big hands gripped the side of the table. "You owe me an explanation." His voice barely reached me.

I swallowed hard. I didn't have any explanations to give. "Soon," I squeaked and cleared my throat, banishing the weakness from my voice. "We'll meet soon."

"We better, Selene. Or I will come for you, the Erlking be damned." The air between us changed and vibrated. The anger faded and was replaced with something far more carnal. He ran his thumb seductively along his lower lip; I wasn't even sure if he was conscious of the motion. His deliberate gaze seared me from my forehead to my fingertips. I didn't blush, but a tingling sensation spread through me as if his fingers followed his eyes. "Should I leave you with a memory?" he asked.

It took everything I had in me not to say please. When I didn't answer, he leaned forward and traced that same thumb over my trembling mouth.

The sun soaked into my skin, melting away all of my concerns about what I was about to do. My toes dug into the soft, white sand. I looked over at Jaron lying next to me. He turned his head in sync with mine. He was always in sync with me and I liked it. I couldn't see the eyes I loved beneath his dark sunglasses, but his permanent 5 o'clock shadow and bold nose made me smile. He reached out and took my hand, pressing a scratchy kiss to the back of my fingers.

"You'll have to behave when you're with the prince," he said lightly, but I knew his feelings were heavy. Jaron didn't like the plan.

"It's the only way."

He dropped my hand and looked forward again. "What if he doesn't like you? Do you have a plan B?"

He hated that I'd be with another man if all went as designed, but it was the best way, the most efficient way, to get what we wanted. Emotions shouldn't factor into it—they certainly wouldn't for the elves. If we wanted to beat the cold, unfeeling fae at their own game, I had no choice but to play dirty. Elves were tricky. They wove lies and partial truths like spiders casting webs to get what they wanted. Jaron taught me that. I had to be ruthless if we were going to win.

"Everybody likes me," I said with a self-assured smile that I didn't feel. "He had to practically pick his jaw up from the ground." I laughed, remembering Cheney's reaction to my trap. Naked and communing with the goddess in the forest he just happened to be hunting in. Men were so easy. A small smile tilted Jaron's mouth before it was smothered with a scowl.

"What do you want from me, Jaron? This is what we planned."

He took off his sunglasses and tossed them into the sand, his intense gray eyes swirling with emotion. "Just make sure you want what you're chasing, Selene. Once it's done, you can't take it back."

I studied him for a moment. Jaron was always threatening to leave me, but he hadn't managed yet. I amended my earlier inner statement: Men were easy, except for Jaron. I abandoned my beach chair and moved over to him, straddling his muscular legs. "That's what you always say."

A small part of me worried he meant it this time, that I might actually go too far, but Jaron had to see that getting my hooks in the king's son was the only way to bring real change. I wasn't doing this for myself. I was doing it for him, for everyone.

He gripped the flare of my hips and pulled me closer. "You'll fall in love with him."

I leaned in, brushing my lips against his. "That's absurd."

He didn't reply. He took possession of my mouth and splayed his hand across my back, pushing me against himself as if he could absorb me. I ran my fingers into his soft waves.

"It will all work out. You'll see," I said when I could speak again.

Jaron had been my anchor for so long, I was afraid of straying too far. He had to know it.

A hand squeezed my shoulder, pulling me out of the memory. "I didn't know he would be here," Femi said.

I blinked and searched the room for Jaron. Had he given me that memory? I shook my head. Not possible. I couldn't jump to conclusions. I wanted to talk about what I remembered, but he was gone. It occurred to me that this was the first memory I had that didn't make me feel physically sick. It was more like a normal memory. It felt like it was part of me and didn't leave me reeling with new, confusing feelings like all others did.

"Where's Jaron?" My voice broke as I spoke.

"That guy? He left. Who is he?" Olivia asked, sitting down with a concerned look.

"It's hard to say," I mumbled, my eyes trailing to the dents his hands left in the side of the table. I looked over at Femi. "Can you call Sy?"

She scrunched her nose. "You can't go home already. This wasn't a girls' night. We didn't do anything fun. We didn't even start a fight."

A man moved near our table, and a sensation similar to the one that had hit me on the dance floor overcame me. If Femi wanted a fight, I could help her with that. I got up and grabbed the man the sensation was coming from and kissed him full on the mouth. Some girl said, "Hey!" but white noise filled my ears and I felt dizzy. The man pulled away and looked at me, then smiled and kissed me back. The feelings flooding into me were incredible. Someone pulled me back, though I fought against them, and Femi stepped in front of me.

"Not for you, jinni."

"She's a big girl. Maybe we should ask her what she wants, Sekhmet?"

Femi made a face at me though I was still feeling swoony. "You want her. You have to go through me."

Olivia squeezed her hand around my wrist, and I immediately began to feel better. "That was impetuous and stupid. Never throw yourself in the line of jinn, unless you can defend yourself against them—and you can't."

"Femi wanted a fight. Now she has a fight."

Olivia grumbled to herself. I watched Femi and the jinni have their standoff. Moments later, after a swift kick to the knee and a lightning fast jab to the throat, the jinni was on the ground and we were headed outside, Femi grinning ear to ear.

"Damn it, Femi," Olivia said when we cleared the building.

"Totally Selene's fault." She winked at me.

TWO

Olivia and I squeezed into Femi's car and she took us back to Sy's. I considered calling Cheney so I could go home, but I needed time to think about what happened with Jaron. When we walked into the Office—a bar that doubled as an unofficial meeting place for anyone with business involving the Abyss—Sy was leaned over the counter talking intimately to a petite girl with black curly hair cascading down her back, big violet eyes, and enviable pouty lips. He glanced up at us and rolled his eyes. "We don't do bachelorette parties," he said dryly.

Femi plopped down on a stool next to the girl and leaned back against the bar, resting her elbows on the ledge. "Who are you?"

"Femi," Sy said with an edge of warning.

"What?" she asked without looking at him, continuing to inspect the woman. "She's not a hunter, and this is a hunter bar. My curiosity is natural."

Sy came around the bar and took the woman's hand. "My apologies, Ligeia. Another night," Sy said smoothly, leading her outside.

Femi chewed on the side of her lip and stared at the door. I glanced at Olivia. She watched Femi, smiling, then took the seat next to her. "You know how to prevent things like that, right?"

Femi blinked and looked at her blankly. "Things like what?"

Olivia groaned. "You're hopeless."

Sy came back and resumed his usual position behind the bar. "That was the fastest girls' night possibly ever. What happened? And what was all that with Ligeia?" He poured us each a drink, then he waited for us to explain.

Femi inspected her sharpened fingernails. "I have no idea what you mean. Am I not allowed to talk to people?"

He frowned. "No, by all means, talk away. Why are you back? You better not be getting my cousin into trouble."

Femi looked up. "You aren't my father, my brother, or even my boyfriend—"

"Whose fault is that?" he tossed out half-heartedly, but he didn't get a smile from her.

"Regardless, I don't have to explain myself to you or anyone."

"We all answer to someone." The intensity built between us until he looked over at Olivia and me. "Right, ladies?"

Olivia's expressive eyes filled with laughter, but she kept her face serious. "The only person I explain myself to is Holden, and I don't even do that very often."

Sy gave them a bemused look. "Selene?" he asked.

I took a deep breath. I actually did want to talk to Sy about what had happened tonight. "I saw Jaron at the club," I said quietly.

He pressed his lips together. "Everybody out," he yelled to the stragglers lurking in the dark corners of the grimy bar. Slowly they trickled out, pulling slips of paper off the wall that looked like wanted posters as they went, and Sy locked the door behind them.

"Holden's on his way," Olivia said.

"I'm here." A deep rumbling voice came from behind us, giving me chills. Holden, as unsettling as always, gave me a cold once-over. "What the fuck is she doing here? I thought you were going out with Femi." Saying he didn't sound pleased was an understatement, but his face softened as he searched Olivia's expression. "Liv?"

Olivia quirked an eyebrow. "Selene's my friend, Sy's cousin, and Femi's friend. Why wouldn't she be here?"

"We're not getting involved in fae politics. Neither of us needs the headache." When Olivia ignored him, Holden rolled his eyes and pulled out his cell phone.

"While everyone's here, you should tell them what happened tonight," Sy said, and I knew he wasn't just talking about my seeing Jaron at the club. He wanted me to tell Olivia and Holden about my studio.

"You can call Cheney if you want," Sy said when I hesitated. Everyone's eyes except for Holden's turned to me.

My center knotted and squeezed at the sound of Cheney's name. "Um, no. No, I don't think so." I took a healthy swig of my drink to numb the pain. From the looks on their faces, I needed to give more of an explanation. "He has a lot going on. I think I can handle this without him." I wanted to talk to Sy about what was going on, not a whole room of people who were practically strangers. I excused myself and walked to the restroom. I washed my hands and took a few deep breaths. I wished I was home, not at the castle, but at my cute little house with my cat where I could call my friends to come over and talk. I dried my hands and shook off the desire. That wasn't my life anymore.

When I returned, Femi, Olivia, and Sy were chatting while Holden stood on the outskirts observing. My hands twisted nervously, and I looked longingly toward the door.

"So, are you going to tell us what's happening or not?" Holden finally asked. Olivia elbowed him and smiled at me.

"If Selene wants our help, she'll ask for it," Olivia said to him. "Let her figure out her own mind."

I shook my head. "I don't know why you're all here. I should go." I couldn't ask these people for help. Just knowing me could prove dangerous.

Femi caught my arm as I moved to leave. "You need their help. It isn't that we won't do what we can, but Sy hardly leaves the bar, and I still have bounties to track. Olivia and Holden have different talents and," her gaze went to Holden, "time on their hands."

Holden gave her a stony look, but she didn't flinch. The idea that Femi hadn't just planned a girls' night—that she'd arranged the get-together specifically to put me into contact with Olivia sans Holden—crossed my mind. Was she making sure they got involved? Tricky, tricky.

"Why don't we give Selene and Sy a little space?" Olivia said.

I smiled at her gratefully, but a knock on the door kept them from leaving. Sy frowned and Holden looked up.

"Baker," he said.

Femi smiled. "Wow, Chuckles, you really rallied the troops."

Holden gave her a level look. "I don't know anything about elves. Baker shoves his nose into everyone else's business. Just like you."

Femi laughed, and a reluctant smile touched Holden's mouth as Sy unlocked the door and let the tough boxer-like redhead in. A trickle of jealousy went through me at the obvious friendship and comfort level among all of them. It made me miss my friends. And it confused me even more. Why would any of them rally anything for me? They didn't know me. Their help made no sense.

Olivia ushered everyone away to a worn out dartboard at the back of the room. Sy sat down next to me and bumped his shoulder against mine. "What's going on up there, coz?" He tapped on his temple. "I thought we were team Cheney."

I rolled my eyes. "Are you 12? I'm not on team anything."

"But I take it from what he said earlier, you haven't told him about Jaron."

I curled the end of the napkin under my drink. "I don't want to bring Jaron up until I can explain everything."

He nodded. "But you can't remember."

I shook my head, fighting tears. "It isn't like I haven't tried. I've done everything. The coven's cast so many spells on me I think I'm getting a brain tumor." Sy laughed and I hit him. "Not funny."

"Maybe you're trying too hard. Maybe if you stop straining, it will come to you."

"I had a memory tonight." I bit my lip, not sure I could bring myself to share this particular memory with Sy. "Normally the memories hurt, but this one didn't."

"What do you mean *hurt*?"

"They give me headaches, make me dizzy, things like that."

"But tonight's didn't? Why? What was different?"

I sighed. "I remembered talking to Jaron. I think it was right after I met Cheney for the first time. But I don't believe it was the memory that was different. I think it was the manner in which it came to me."

He raised his eyebrows.

"Jaron asked if I wanted a memory, then he touched me and immediately it started playing."

Sy stood up, poured himself a drink, and sat back down. "You and Jaron were together before you met Cheney? That lends some credibility to his claim that you started the rebellion."

I nodded miserably. "But if I was with him, why don't you know about it?"

He shook his head. "You didn't come around a lot, and when you did, you always came alone. Hell, I heard more about your life from rumors than I ever did from you. How do you feel about Jaron now?"

Conflicted. Attracted. In over my head. "I don't know. It feels like I'm being torn in two. I need Cheney like air, but there's something about Jaron." I let out a ragged breath. "He could have taken Michael for all I know."

"You really think he has something to do with Michael's disappearance? It does seem a little convenient that he found you that easily the one night you're away from Cheney."

I nodded.

"Okay," Sy said slowly. "Talk to Jaron about what happened before you left. You've heard Cheney's side of things, and I admit it's compelling when it stands alone—but maybe there's a whole lot he left out. See what Jaron knows. Then figure out what you want. It doesn't matter what you wanted then—only what you want *now*. You're the one living the rest of your life."

I nodded.

"I've said it before, but I think you should move in here until you figure out what's going on. The longer you stay with Cheney, the harder it will be to leave if you decide you want to."

"I can't. I told him I wouldn't run away from him again, and I'm not going to. Besides, we're bonded. I don't know if I can leave him for an extended period of time."

"Then bite the bullet and tell him what's happening. See how the dice fall." He patted my leg. "You should tell them everything." He nodded toward Femi and her friends. "Right now you don't know who to trust in the fae world, but none of them are connected to any of this. You can trust them."

I watched them play. Holden was the only one to look up and meet my eyes. "Even Holden?"

"Well, if Olivia likes you, he probably won't hurt you. He might even have some insight on who would've burned down your studio—and on whether Michael's alive."

As much as I didn't feel like doing it, I agreed, and Sy called everyone back.

"You guys pretty much know Cheney's side of events," I started, "but it turns out everything isn't quite as simple as that."

"It never is," Olivia said.

"I don't know any of these names. Who's this cat, Cheney? Is he the one who was staring daggers at that vamp?" Baker said.

Holden gave him an evil look, but then he said, "You should fill him in on everything. Despite being relentlessly annoying, he knows a lot about the races."

Baker grinned and I shrugged. "Cheney's the son of the former Erlking and the current ruler of the fae. A few months ago I didn't know I was anything other than a human witch. Then Cheney came to find me. He told me the rebels were after me, his father had a bounty on me, and that I was bound to him. From that moment on I've been stuck in this stupid world. No offense." I got a few faint smiles, but everyone waited for me to continue. "I was a half-elf and I became a changeling by choice. Cheney said I did it to stop the rebels, but now I'm not so sure. Femi found the rebel leader, a half-elf named Jaron. He claims I helped him start the movement. It appears I also had a relationship with him."

I ran my fingers through my hair and summed up the more recent events, starting with Cheney overthrowing his father and ending with talking to Jaron tonight. "So that's what's happening."

Holden looked at Olivia, his eyes burning. "You went to a jinn club."

She shrugged and took his hand. "It wasn't a big deal. No one noticed me, I swear."

"This isn't over." He kissed the back of her hand and looked back to me. "Forget your love life. Your main problem is someone's trying to kill you." His voice was flat and he seemed perfectly indifferent about it.

My mouth fell open, unsure how to respond. Yes, my studio was demolished and Michael was missing, but it seemed like a leap to assume those things meant someone wanted me dead.

"If they were trying to kill her, they're stupid," Femi said. "Why would they burn down a building she hasn't even been in for months and abduct one of her friends?"

Holden sighed, but Baker spoke up. "It's not like that, minx. The boss-man's right. Selene's been living in a palace, next to impossible to get to. This little stunt pulled her out into the open. Put her back on the playing field. Makes it clear that if she hides, what she loves will be at risk."

"But why?" I asked.

"Beats me. You're hot, but no dame's worth all that fuss." Baker winked. "Maybe the person knows your involvement with the rebels."

"Do you think it was Jaron? If someone wanted to draw me out, he's the one who followed me from the studio to the club."

"Could be," Holden said. "Could also be Cheney."

"Why Cheney?" Sy asked.

"To keep her in her place. She said herself she has a history of running away. You can't run away if you have nowhere to go. And the ex just makes everything that much more real. Keeps the threat level high and her needing his protection."

That notion sunk like a lead brick in my stomach. Cheney wouldn't do that, would he? "Do you think Michael's still alive?"

"I'd keep him alive. So long as he lives and you care, they've got you by the short hairs."

"Cheney wouldn't do that."

"Look, you already know he's lied to you, or at the very least, told you only partial truths. Don't take him off the suspect list until you can be certain." Holden stared off into nothing. "Then again, it could be practically anyone you pissed off in what I'm assuming was your significant lifetime before you were reborn. Do you have any notion of other enemies?"

Only two came to mind. "Alanna. She's fae, and she and Cheney were together until I popped back into the picture. She sort of hates me. And Cheney's father. He'd love to see me dead—and most of the full elves wouldn't weep at my funeral either. "

"Cheney has plenty of enemies too," Sy pointed out.

Olivia shook her head. "Burning down her studio and taking her ex-fiancé seems like a personal attack on Selene. I don't think Cheney's enemies factor in. Where's Cheney's father?"

"I don't know where they took him. Cheney had him removed after he took the crown."

"Worth looking into," Baker said.

"Okay." Femi slapped her hands together. "I'll tail Jaron since I already found him. Baker, you see what you can find on Alanna. Sy, ask around and see what the fae community is feeling about Selene these days. Olivia and Holden, will you check out the scene and see if I missed anything that might be of use and see if you can get a lead on where the human's being kept?"

"Sure," Olivia said. "And I'll do a scan for Michael tomorrow. Maybe something will come through the guardian lines if he's a human in need of help."

"What am I supposed to do?" I asked.

"Just keep being pretty." Femi gave me an ornery smile when I glared at her. "I'm serious. You need to keep doing what you've been doing. Don't let Cheney know anything's different until he's in the clear. And I think you should meet with Jaron. It's time we heard his side. But if you're really itching for a task, find out where Cheney's keeping his dad."

I could do that. "Thank you all." I looked at each of them in turn.

"Don't thank us yet, doll. We haven't done anything. Just keep your eyes open, and let us know if any change starts rattlin' the old noggin." Baker stood up and hugged me until Sy told him to move along.

One by one, they all left. I looked at Sy. "Do you really think Cheney's trying to trap me?"

Sy rolled his neck. "I don't know. I'd like to think he's different than his family, but he secretly married you before you became a changeling. It's all a matter of timing. Did he marry you before or after you lost your memory? If the latter, I don't know what reason he'd have except to trap you."

"He could've done it to protect me."

Sy gave me a dubious look. "That's one way to see it."

THREE

Cheney was business as usual the next day. He woke me up and handed me my favorite green smoothie. "If you don't get up, you'll be late for training."

Cheney and Sebastian decided I needed to continue to train until I was as proficient in everything as I had been or I had my memory back. "I have more important things to worry about than training right now," I grumbled.

He kissed my temple. "Nothing is more important than training. It keeps you alive." He pulled the covers off and roused me from bed. "Your friends will all be here this afternoon," he said conversationally.

I sighed and walked into the bathroom. "I don't want them to feel like prisoners."

"They won't," he said from the doorway. "It's the only way I know how to keep them safe."

"What about Gram?"

He shook his head. "She refused to come. I've assigned her a bodyguard."

"You could do that for them, too." Even though they all agreed to come here, somewhat willingly, I couldn't imagine upheaving so many lives.

"If you'd prefer–"

I nodded. "At least I can give them a choice." I dressed quickly and called all of the coven. Everyone, except Katrina, decided to have a bodyguard. Kat, in her own words, said, "Hell no. I'm blowing this popsicle stand. I've been packed and waiting on my porch since I hung up the phone last night."

I couldn't help but laugh. I let Cheney know the new plan then headed down to Sebastian. He was reading a book when I came in.

"I wasn't sure you'd make it today," he said without looking up.

"I'm only a couple minutes late." I sat down next to him. "What cruel and unusual punishment do you have for me today?"

He snapped the book closed. "My comment has nothing to do with you being late. Cheney told me what happened last night. I'm very sorry, Selene."

Worry crept back in. I'd been so preoccupied with disrupting my friends' lives I'd forgotten about Michael. "Do you think he's still alive?"

Sebastian's serious eyes met mine. "I think you have every reason to hope."

"Cheney isn't going to help look for him."

Sebastian nodded. "He has many obligations–"

"That's bullshit and you know it."

"Regardless of what he may or may not want to do, he has a responsibility to his people as well as to you. He's walking a tight rope, trying to keep everyone happy. Don't make it any harder on him."

I moved down to the floor and began stretching. "So if there was something that might have happened in the past that would upset Cheney, should I wait to tell him?"

Sebastian was silent for so long I looked up to make sure he was still in the room. He stared at me, his face unreadable. "Like what?"

I shrugged. "Just a general question in case I have any more memories."

"Did you have a memory?"

"Of course not." He didn't look convinced. "I would tell you if I did." Sebastian nodded and offered me a hand to help me up. "You never answered my question."

"I guess it depends on whether or not what you remember changes how you feel about things now."

"What do you mean?"

"If a memory alters how you feel about Cheney, he deserves to know. If it doesn't, then I wouldn't worry about it. You both made mistakes. The past should be left in the past."

Did Sebastian already know my involvement with the rebels? I couldn't ask without giving myself away, but I was tempted. "So you're advocating secret keeping?"

"No, I'm just saying you should keep things between the two of you as simple as possible. You already have plenty of obstacles. If you don't need to add to them, don't."

I took his hand and stood. "I'll keep that in mind."

Sebastian led me outside to a hedge maze. He waved his hand toward it. "Get to the center."

I peered in. "What did you do to it? What's in there waiting to kill me?"

He smiled. "Nothing will kill you. See you in the center." He disappeared, and I rolled my shoulders back. I could do this.

I picked up the quarterstaff leaning next to the entrance. The hedge's gnarled pine walls were almost twice my height and as wide as my arm span. I got to the first wall and had a choice: left or right. The two paths looked identical.

"I hate mazes," I muttered. The creaking and popping of branches around me made me jump. I looked behind me; the entrance to the labyrinth was gone, the path I'd just followed nothing but shrubbery. "Damn it."

If I couldn't go back, I couldn't afford to make the wrong decision. How was I supposed to know which way to go? While I stood there contemplating the greenery groaned and trembled. Suddenly it came to me. I was making this unnecessarily complicated. I shook my head and mustered my energy. I needed to get to the middle, so I'd walk a straight path. I parted the hedges like the red sea, stepped over a multitude of roots, and walked easily to Sebastian. He closed his book and stood when I arrived.

"Well done. And what did you learn from this exercise?"

"You're an ass who was trying to trap me in a hedge for hours?"

He raised his eyebrows. "No. There was no wrong choice in this maze. Any direction you took would've led you here, but you chose not to take the established trails. You made your own way. Why?"

I thought about it. "I didn't know which way to go, and I didn't want to make a mistake."

"Mistakes are inevitable. All you can do is deal with them."

"Hmph. So is this the only thing we're doing today?"

He nodded. "Find your way out and you are finished."

"Cool." I collected my energy again, but this time the

hedge didn't budge. I looked behind me. Sebastian smiled.

"This maze is designed to keep people in. It adjusts. Now that it's aware of your ability, it is immune to it. The two established trails are blocked because of your method. Good luck." He disappeared before I could say anything.

I spun in a slow circle. Sure enough, there were no openings. Had I chosen right or left, only that path would've closed and I could've taken the other one out, but since I made my own way, I lost those options. How the hell was I supposed to get out? I paced the square area, thinking. There had to be a way. If I could transport like every other elf in the world, it would be no problem, but I couldn't. I could tear down a house without breaking a sweat. An enchanted maze wasn't going to defeat me. I let my frustration build and dug up my anger, confusion, and worry until it felt like my skin was vibrating and the ground beneath my feet shook. If I couldn't make the hedges move, then I had to get rid of them. I lifted the dirt beneath each bush, forcing them up and out of the ground. The branches scratched and poked me as I climbed out, but I made it to where Sebastian was waiting. He looked at the destruction behind me with wide eyes.

"That's one way to do it."

"There was no other way."

He opened his mouth to say something and everything went black.

I was lounging on the bench in the center of the hedge maze, staring up at the night sky and waiting for Cheney. Jasmine from the garden drifted in the breeze and made a strand of my hair flutter. Someday this would be mine. I would be welcome here.

"You ready?" Cheney's voice came from above me.

I smiled, not looking at him. "No. Do you ever just enjoy all of this? You have so much, but you never stop and see it."

"I don't enjoy it? You hate it here."

"No, I hate it in there." I pointed in the direction of the palace. "I like it here."

He picked up my feet and sat on the bench, resting my legs across his. "My dad will come around. We just have to give him time."

My relaxation began to dissolve. "I don't want to talk about your father."

"Well, the two of you have that in common. He doesn't want to talk about you either."

This was all so much harder than I'd thought it would be. "Why do you like me?"

"What?" he said with a half laugh.

"Why do you like me? We're so different. Your life would be so much easier without me."

"I've had an easy life and I can tell you one thing for certain. I would rather fight with you than be anywhere else."

"What if I'm not always here?"

"I will always find you." He patted my leg. "This sort of talk is ridiculous. Don't let my father get in your head. So long as we both love one another, we will always find a way to be together."

A flood of sticky warmth flowing down over my mouth woke me up. I retched and my stomach rolled over and heaved out my breakfast. It mixed with the blood pouring from my nose. It felt like I'd been hit with a bat.

"Are you okay?" Sebastian's voice drifted into my thoughts.

"Do I look okay?" I croaked.

"Get Cheney," he said to someone.

I braced my arms against the ground as my stomach continued to purge itself.

"Another memory," Sebastian said.

"They're getting worse. You said they wouldn't keep getting worse," Cheney said as he reached down and scooped my hair out of my face.

"That was my best guess."

"This has to stop. Before they kill her."

When I was confident I had nothing left in my stomach, I rolled over onto my back, letting the cool air wash over my face. "Who's going to kill me now?"

Cheney knelt beside me and ran a damp cloth over my face. "No one. What did you remember this time?"

"Us, talking in the maze after you spoke to your father."

He smiled. "I remember that. I told you we'd find a way to be together. I was right." His eyes flickered to the maze. "What the hell happened there?"

I covered my eyes with my arm to block out the light. "I got out."

"I can see that." He chuckled. "Let's get you back inside." He gently lifted me to him and a moment later I felt him lower me onto the bed.

"We can't stop the memories, Cheney. Too many spells have been cast. We didn't let things happen naturally. They're going to keep coming."

"Maybe we can repress them again."

I shook my head. "No more spells. I need to remember. I

want to remember. Let's just hope it doesn't kill me."

"Memories don't kill people."

"Memories don't make most people bleed." I bit my lip and tried to think of a good way to bring up what had been on my mind since he took the throne. "Maybe we should try to break the bond."

Cheney lifted my arm from my eyes. "What are you saying?"

"I don't need the protection of the bond anymore, and it won't change anything between us, right? I'm tired of everything in my life being riddled with magic. I want to feel my own *real* feelings and remember in my own time. You must understand that."

He looked back toward the door. "It's not possible. This sort of bond can't be broken."

"It's just magic, Cheney. Any spell can be broken." I took his hand. "Please consider it."

"We'll see." He kissed my forehead. "I have to get back to work. Are you okay?"

I nodded. "Fine."

FOUR

"Why are you in bed?" Katrina's voice made me smile. My headache was all but gone. "I've been waiting and waiting for, like, ever." She plopped down on the edge of my bed. "Entertain me, monkey."

"When did you get here?" I sat up, stretching my arms over my head.

"About an hour ago. Oh my gosh, you should see the room Cheney put me in. Swank. I think *I* might be in love with him."

I laughed. "Good lord, don't tell him that. That's the last thing his ego needs."

"So why are you in bed?" she repeated. "Are you sick? Is that blood?" She leaned in closer, pointing at the left side of my mouth.

I wiped my thumb across the corner of my lips. "Yeah. I had a memory."

Her eyebrows pulled together. "And you blacked out and hit your head?"

"No. They just … some of them can be painful."

Her mouth fell open. "Then why the hell are we casting spells to make you remember?"

I swung my legs over the edge of the bed and stood up.

"I need to remember, Kat. There isn't a choice."

"Sure there is. Who cares what happened? You have a nice, smoking hot husband who looks at you like you walk on water, you live in a freaking castle, and you have the greatest friends in the world. You don't need to remember jack."

"I'm not trying to remember Jack. I am trying to remember Selene."

"Ha ha," she said. "Funny."

I shrugged and nodded toward the door. "You want to see the castle?"

"Hell yeah." She followed me out of the room.

I walked her through the wings I was familiar with, but the more we saw the quieter she became. "What's wrong with you?" I said.

"You're too fancy for us now. I'm afraid to touch anything. I might break it and your husband will kick me out and then you'll forget us little people."

I laughed. "I assure you I'm the same as I ever was. You've been here before."

"Yeah, but I didn't see the library or the billiard room or ballroom or–"

I waved her off. "Yeah, yeah, I get it. That isn't me though." I slung my arm over her shoulder. "I think we could use a drink."

"Yes. Liquor me up and find a handsome elf to take advantage of me."

I laughed again.

"The two of you are having far too much fun. Surely we can find work for you to do," Sebastian said behind us.

"Hey, Sebastian. How have you been?" Katrina gave

him a half wave.

He cleared his throat. "Very well, thank you." Sebastian folded his hands behind his back then released them, shifting his weight from one foot to the other. "I see our queen is doing much better with you here."

What on earth had gotten into Sebastian? "I've been perfectly fine."

His voice returned to normal when he looked at me. "If by 'fine' you mean sulking. I haven't heard you laugh like that for—"

"Weeks," Cheney supplied, coming from the other direction. "I'm glad to see you arrived safely, Katrina." He gave her a bow and ran his hand down my arm, twining his fingers with mine. "Where are the two of you headed?"

"I'm about to get her liquored up and find her a—" Katrina stomped on my foot and I stifled a laugh.

Sebastian and Cheney gave us odd looks.

"Would the two of you be interested in dinner?" Sebastian said, his eyes lingering on Katrina.

I glanced at Cheney and an almost imperceptible smile tilted his lips. "Dinner is a wonderful idea, Sebastian," he said, tugging my hand, leading me down the hallway toward the dining room.

"Sebastian is acting weird," I said loud enough for only Cheney to hear.

Cheney nodded. "You don't think he likes …" He raised an eyebrow.

I glanced behind us. Sebastian and Kat were walking side by side, and Kat was describing her favorite sitcom in detail and randomly tossing out quotes. Sebastian's hands were once again folded behind his back, and his eyes were trained to the floor. "They have nothing in common."

Cheney shrugged. "I've known him a long time and I've never seen him invite anyone to dinner."

I smiled. "They'd be sort of cute together."

Cheney's eyes flickered to mine. "Until she grows old and leaves him to carry on alone for thousands of years. It cannot work between humans and elves. It is best that races maintain some ... distance." There was an ever-so-slight disapproving tone to his voice.

My smile melted away and I looked at my feet. My friends would all grow old and leave me. Was this Cheney's way of telling me I should distance myself from them? It wasn't going to happen. "What's that supposed to mean?" I struggled to keep my voice relaxed.

Cheney shook his head. "Just that Sebastian knows better than to set his sights on a human girl. Don't get your hopes up—or hers."

I forced a smile. "Just like you knew better than to set your sights on a half-elf?"

His chin lifted slightly. "That wasn't meant to be a statement about us."

I pushed back my irritation. "Let me make one more point then I'll drop it." He watched me cautiously. "If elves and humans were never together, I wouldn't be here."

He blinked a couple times, and I let go of his hand and took a seat at the huge table. We'd have to shout to talk to each other. I was about to say something when Sebastian seemed to arrive at the same conclusion.

"Why don't we sit in the garden?" he suggested.

"Wonderful idea," I said and smiled as I stood. Katrina and Sebastian headed out of the opulent room. Cheney caught my arm before I could make it to the door.

"I didn't think about it like that. It isn't like I would prevent the romance if they chose it. It's just—"

I raised an eyebrow. "More trouble than it's worth?"

His eyes narrowed. "I can't win this discussion with you, can I?"

"Your actions have to reflect what you say you believe, or you'll never unite the people. Sebastian's your biggest supporter. You've sold him on this idea that all of us are the same. You can't take it back just because he decides he likes a human."

"Maybe he's just being polite. You may have started an argument for no reason." He put his hand on my waist as we walked toward the door.

"Or maybe Katrina has no interest in him."

"Now you just want to argue."

I laughed and he pulled me to a stop. "I'll think about what you said—and you see? This is why I need you." His lips brushed against mine. "Why we shouldn't break the bond."

I pulled back. "But the bond was just a precaution. We were together before it. We'll still be together after, right?"

"Let's hope we never have to find out. Come on. We've kept them waiting long enough."

"Tonight was fun," Katrina said, stretching across her bed. "But you haven't told me what's happening. Why did I move to the castle? Why do the others have bodyguards?

And what happened to your studio?"

"Someone set it on fire." I traced an invisible pattern on the comforter. "And took Michael."

"What?" She sat up, covering her mouth. "How do you know?"

I told her what I knew to this point.

"Well, you'll find him. You must be so worried." She squeezed my hand.

"But now you see why I need to remember my past. Or things like this will keep happening." I swallowed hard. I still hadn't mentioned Jaron because I didn't know what to say. "There's more. I think I'm responsible for all of this."

"What do you mean?"

I leaned in close to her. "I might have started the rebellion."

Her brown eyes met mine, wide and uncertain. "Does Cheney know?"

"No."

She whistled and sat back. "Holy crap on cracker. We need to get the others here."

"No. They're safer where they are."

"Not for them, silly. For you. You've been keeping far too many secrets for too long. If you ever needed us, it's now."

I shook my head. "Not yet. We'll visit Sy tomorrow after the coven goes home. Hopefully his friends have found something. I don't want to involve any of you further, until I know for certain where I stand." Kat frowned and looked like she was going to object. "Don't say anything to anyone."

She nodded. "Fine, but I don't want to be a spectator in this. If you shut me out, I'll start blabbing. And you know I like to talk."

I gave her a quick hug. "I'm glad you're here."

FIVE

The next day all the girls came for our regular practice with Gram's Book of Shadows. They distracted me from the worry that ate around the edge of my mind. After we finished, I showered and dressed, getting ready to make an excuse to Cheney about why I needed to see Sy.

"Good, you're ready." Cheney pulled off his shirt as I walked out.

"I am. Did we have plans?"

"We're meeting with Paolo tonight. I told you that, right?"

I shook my head. Seeing Sy would have to wait. Paolo was the closest thing to a leader the vampires had. If he and Cheney had finally come to an agreement on a time and place to meet, I had to be there. Paolo's second in command, Corbin, insisted—I may have flirted with him a bit the first time we met—that I attend all meetings with the vampires, and Paolo had held firm on that point. Sebastian's intel said the rebels were trying to recruit the vampires by offering them a seat in the fae court, but Cheney didn't think the vampires wanted that. What they really wanted was to be part of the Hunt—something only Cheney, as the new Erlking, could offer them. I was informed in no uncertain terms by

Cheney and Sebastian that my part in this was to sit by Cheney and look pretty—not talk. They were afraid I would either irritate the vampires or draw too much interest. I seemed to have that way about me.

I looked down at my jeans and hoodie, not exactly business appropriate. I turned back toward the closet.

"Where are you going?" Cheney said.

"I have to change," I called back. I opted for black pants, a gold belted tank top, and a black blazer. I looked respectable and a bit queenlier. When I came out of our room, he was gone. I found him in the study talking with Katrina.

Kat looked up when I entered. Then she glanced down at her own jeans and sweatshirt. "Do I need to change?" she asked.

"No. We have to postpone tonight. I have a meeting to go to with Cheney. Is that okay?"

"Sure. I'll find Sebastian and see what he's up to. Or maybe catch up on some reading."

"Do you remember where the library is?" I asked, coming to a stop in front of Cheney, so close that his legs touched mine. What can I say, I was an addict and he was my favorite drug. He was lucky I didn't sit on his lap. "What were you two talking about?"

"I was telling him about my new and improved abilities."

I smiled to cover the frown. All of my friends were slowly but surely changing, and it was my fault. I hated to see it happen. I didn't want them to get hurt in any of this. Cheney stood up. "It was nice talking to you. I'm sure Sebastian will be more than happy to entertain you if you get bored."

I waved at her. "We have a date with some vampires."

The vampire lair was nothing like I imagined. I thought it would be dark and gothic with heavily draped walls, a chandelier perhaps, and candelabras ... lots of candelabras actually. Oh, and a butler, too. So maybe I'd seen too many movies, because the "lair" was nothing like that. It wasn't a gothic mansion, nothing had a grayish, cold tint, and there wasn't a coffin in sight.

The nest was a Cape Cod-style house with three perfect white dormer windows, a manicured lawn with a trellis of pink roses, and a large porch that begged to be sat on with an iced tea and a good book. Now this was a vampire I had to meet.

Cheney's knock was firm and quick. Almost instantly the door opened, revealing a tall, thin man with dark hair and a dignified posture. He smiled and his face lit up. "You must be the Erlking, and you must be Selene. Welcome to my home," he said with a heavy English accent, which threw me for a loop. I expected him to be Spanish. He gave us a welcoming gesture.

Cheney bowed and I smiled. "Thank you. It's wonderful meeting you."

"And you, Selene. I've heard much of you from Corbin. He is quite besotted, though I fear his infatuation may be a hopeless cause." He glanced to Cheney with an apologetic smile. "Corbin will behave himself. You have my word as a gentleman."

The last time I met Corbin he fed on me without my knowing it because Cheney had failed to mention that vampires could feed by touch. Now Cheney took exception to everything about Corbin where I was concerned, but I was more confident I could take care of myself this time.

"Stealing her affections does not concern me. Feeding off of her is another story."

"Not even a taste," our host said stoically. "Now please come in. Dinner is almost ready. It's a rare pleasure to have guests who actually eat food, and yet I've developed a passion for cooking." He ushered us to the dining room where the table was elaborately set with service for eight. When we were settled, Paolo excused himself and hurried to the kitchen.

"This is weird, right?" I whispered.

Cheney squeezed my hand. "It's all new to me."

"He seems nice."

"Pay attention and tread lightly."

"Selene, love, how wonderful to see you again." Corbin walked into the room with a smile, his eyes focused on me. "I would kiss your hand, but I'm not allowed to touch you."

I stifled a laugh, knowing Cheney wouldn't appreciate it. "It's nice seeing you again, too. You remember Cheney?"

Corbin nodded to him. "You seemed a bit testy with our girl Selene when we last met. I hope you didn't hurt her or we'll have a problem, mate."

Cheney gave him a cold glare. "I would never hurt—or feed on—her."

Corbin turned his gaze back to me. "That was bad form. I apologize, love. But it did seem like you were offering."

"Yes, well, this isn't an awkward subject at all." I made a face at both of them. How was I supposed to explain why I didn't know how vampires fed when I couldn't tell anyone I didn't have a memory? Cheney's hand rested on my knee. He of all people should know better than to bring it up.

"Selene's quite right. We shouldn't talk about anything that makes my guests uncomfortable," Paolo said, walking in, balancing several dishes of food. Maybe it was just me, but I had the feeling he was either fattening us up like the witch in Hansel and Gretel, or he really wanted a non-vampire friend. Paolo disappeared back into the kitchen, only to return with even more food.

"Tuck in. Help yourselves." Everything smelled wonderful, but none of the men made a move toward the dishes, so I did. I took a small sample of everything, not wanting to be rude. Paolo smiled encouragingly and served himself, too. Did vampires eat real food? Cheney and Corbin followed suit reluctantly.

"What do you do, Selene?" Paolo asked, watching every bite that entered my mouth, making me worry it was drugged or poisoned.

"I own a yoga studio," I said automatically, not thinking about the fact it had burned down or that I was now queen of the fae.

"You say these things to torture me, don't you, love?" Corbin said with a glint in his eyes.

Cheney didn't react, probably trying to think of how to cover up my faux pas rather than worrying about Corbin. However, Paolo gave Corbin a look that could have withered flowers. He was a scary, scary man underneath the warm and fuzzy exterior.

"What about you, Paolo? What did you do before you were a vampire?" I asked. Cheney squeezed my leg in warning. I bit my lip. I forgot I wasn't supposed to talk. "I'm sorry. Was that rude?" I asked immediately.

"Not at all. Very few people ask me about my human days, but I quite enjoy talking about it. I was a carpenter. It was my passion."

"Do you still build?"

"Actually, I do. If you come with me, I'll show you."

"Oh ..." I glanced at Cheney. I'd sworn I wouldn't leave his side, but since I'd brought up the topic, it would be rude to say no. Political maneuvering was proving to be way too much for me to handle.

Paolo noticed my hesitation. "I swear by my life, Erlking, no harm will come to her tonight in my home."

Cheney smiled diplomatically and nodded to me. I stood up from my chair, still not entirely certain this is what he had in mind. Paolo walked me to a guest bedroom and nodded toward the door. I went in, showing no fear or hesitation.

"You're not frightened of me, are you." he said, but it was more a thoughtful statement than a question.

"I have no doubt you're very dangerous, but no, I'm not scared of you."

He leaned against the doorjamb. "Why not?"

"I've done nothing to make you want to hurt me. You seem smarter than that."

"Vampires do not need reasons. We are barely above werewolves, are we not?"

I pressed my lips together, then I took a breath before I spoke. "I guess that depends."

"On what?"

"Your actions. Tonight you've been the perfect host. I would be far more nervous about being in a room alone with my human grandmother than you."

Paolo laughed loudly, looking pleased. "This is my latest project." He vaguely gestured at nothing in particular.

"Which piece?"

"All of them." I looked at the bedroom set. It was marvelous.

"May I?" I asked, my hands hovering at the drawer of the dresser.

"Please," he said, nodding encouragingly. I opened the drawer smoothly. It was built with masterful precision.

"This is beautiful."

"I would hope so. I've been doing this for around a thousand years."

I swallowed hard. I knew he was old, but that old never ever crossed my mind. I wasn't sure what the appropriate response was. "I imagine the world has changed quite a bit in that time."

"If you don't count technology, surprisingly little."

"How did you become a vampire?"

"I was made by my lover."

Corbin had said Cheney was more his type than I was, so I took a chance. "And where is he?"

"He was killed."

"I'm sorry," I said, taking his hand on sympathy without thinking. Paolo looked down at our joined fingers. He didn't move, but I could see something flickering in his eyes. He took a labored breath then let it out slowly.

"It was long ago."

If vampires had a bond anything like the magical one

Cheney and I had, it wouldn't matter how long ago it was. It had to hurt him every day. "Time doesn't heal everything."

"No, it doesn't," he said, looking at me curiously. "I can say with some amount of certainty I have never met anyone like you, Selene Warren. You're open and kind, yet bold and fearless—and there's something else deep in your eyes ... something begging to be wild and free."

"I think that's the elf," I said offhandedly.

"Do you ever let her come out and play?" I shook my head. "And yet the Erlking loves you. Curious."

I looked back at the furniture, not knowing what else to say.

"Do you love him?"

I began coughing. I had no idea how I felt. I was attracted to Cheney, but we were also bonded. How much of what I felt was real when someone like Jaron could take my breath away with a one dark stare?

"Even more curious. Which half is unsure, Selene?"

"I'm still figuring things out."

"Is that so?"

"Have no doubts about my affection for Cheney. Even being away from him now pains me."

Paolo removed his hand from mine and patted my shoulder. "Then we should go back. I do not wish to cause either of you pain."

I smiled at Cheney when I sat down to reassure him I was fine. Beneath the table, his hand found my leg, rubbing small circles just above my knee. We continued on with our meal, Paolo never brought up the matter of business. When dinner was over, I helped him clear the dishes and we all went to the living room.

"I like both of you," Paolo said with finality. "However, I cannot involve my people in a war simply because I like you."

Cheney nodded slowly. "I understand that."

Paolo drummed his fingers in front of him like Mr. Burns from the Simpsons, which would have made me smile except I was crushed by his revelation that they wouldn't help. "What can you offer the vampires?"

"What do you require?" Cheney asked.

"No more than your friendship, which you have demonstrated yourself capable of giving. You ate with me, you allowed me to be alone with Selene, and you spoke with me as a friend and not just a piece on a chess board. Others will not be swayed by such gestures. Corbin was moved to help you by meeting Selene. Again, everyone would not be so, nor would you want them to be. What can you offer them?"

"It's my understanding the rebels offered you a place in the fae."

"Perhaps," Paolo said, showing no emotion about the offer.

"I'm not going to offer that. I have no memory of the vampires ever wanting to be anything other than autonomous. I will, however, give you something no one else can. A place in the Hunt."

Paolo leaned back in his chair as he considered the offer. "That could work. There has been interest in participating for a couple centuries. You would do this?"

Cheney nodded.

"I will present the idea and see if they're willing. Regardless of what the other vampires choose, you have my support," Paolo said, standing.

Cheney stood as well, shaking his hand. "I do not need anything from you just yet. I want to get my kingdom in order before I move against the rebels."

"Understood. If there is anything else I can assist you with, please call."

Corbin winked at me. I hopped up and threw my arms around Paolo. "Thank you," I said, kissing him on the cheek. Paolo stiffened but lightly returned the hug. When I pulled back, Cheney had a horrified look on his face.

Paolo laughed. "There's no one quite like you, Selene, but I fear I must forgive Corbin for his infraction while speaking with you. I too am having a hard time resisting when so much life and energy pours forth." He spoke calmly, but his eyes glowed like charcoal embers.

"Sorry," I said, trying not to stare. "I got caught up in the moment."

Paolo blinked a few times until his eyes were back to normal. "Never change, my dear. It has been a very long time since I was hugged. I rather enjoyed it."

"Where's my hug?" Corbin asked, standing up. Cheney placed an unnecessary restraining hand on my waist.

"With your self-control," I told him sweetly, causing both vampires to laugh.

They were dangerous and they could kill me, but I really liked both of them and I told Cheney so when we left. He shook his head. "You hugged a vampire after everything I told you. You *hugged* him. That's like waving a glass of water in front of a person dying of thirst."

"I wasn't thinking. I was excited they're going to help."

"One of these days your cute, bumbling charm isn't

going to work and you're going to be in serious trouble."

"Maybe so, but for right now I'm doing pretty well, if I do say so myself."

"You haven't been bitten yet, but I wouldn't keep testing the waters. There are plenty of fish who would be more than happy to swallow you whole."

"But you'll come to my aid." I smiled at him.

"Nothing could stop me."

"Then I don't have anything to worry about." I squeezed his arm.

The thought that the vampires might help me find Michael crossed my mind, but I didn't want to jeopardize Cheney's plan by asking more of them. I had fun tonight, and I was glad Cheney was getting the kingdom lined up like he wanted to, but I had more important things to worry about. Not only was Michael depending on me, but I had another new idea. If I was the leader of the rebels, perhaps I could stop them and save everyone.

SIX

Cheney and I squared off in the gymnasium for our daily sparing while Sebastian watched from the sidelines. Cheney held a curved scimitar that moved so fast it blurred. I twirled a cusped falchion, a sword with a long, straight blade with a curved tip, in my hand, waiting for an opening while he showed off.

"Any day now," Sebastian said.

I held my form. I couldn't beat his strength or speed. Patience was the key. Cheney glided closer, still spinning the sword in a dizzying pattern. Finally I saw it, the flaw in his design. When the opportunity arose I moved faster than humanly possible. Cheney stopped—the tip of my sword pressed against his chest over his heart. Sebastian clapped.

"And what did we learn today?"

"Show-offs never win," I told him with a grin.

Sebastian gave me a rare smile. "That, and patience is the best strategy in every battle. Let your opponent make their own mistakes. We just might make a queen out of you yet."

"Wouldn't count on it." I twirled my sword with nimble fingers as I walked toward him. "But we won't be fighting in any battles in the near future, will we? The king is gone. The rebels haven't done anything we can prove. So why am I still being trained? We could use this time to find whoever took Michael."

Sebastian's eyes drifted to Cheney and I followed his gaze. "What?" Neither of them replied. "What are you not telling me?"

Cheney sighed. "I think we should eliminate the rebels before they cause any more trouble."

I let that sink in. "But what if they're giving you time to prove you won't be the man your father was? There could be a peaceful end to all of this."

"It is the smart choice to eradicate the enemy when they are not prepared for you," Sebastian said.

"They're not the enemy. They're people, half-elves like me, who were treated unfairly. You both said that. They wanted change, demanded change, and now they have it. We should heal."

Cheney crossed his arms over his chest. "We will heal. But those who made the situation worse will be punished or exiled."

I dropped my weapon. It made a clanging sound as it hit the floor. "I won't train for that."

"Sebastian and I have discussed this many times, Selene. I would love to let the past go, but we have to show our strength now, or we'll suffer the consequences later. If we display our power, we will not be challenged lightly in the future. We'll still do everything we discussed. We will unite the fae, give everyone a say on the council. We just have to punish the people who took part in the rebellion."

I left the gym, not wanting to hear any more and not trusting myself not to say if they were looking for someone to punish they should look no further than me. *Damn it.* I went to my room and changed into jeans and a t-shirt. Cheney wasn't far behind me.

"Selene—"

"Don't you Selene me." I yanked out my ponytail holder and ran my fingers through my hair. "I don't want to talk about this now. Kat and I are going to visit Sy."

"You can't tell them about our plans."

I frowned. "You have Sebastian to talk to, but I can't talk to anyone. How is that fair?"

He put his hands on my shoulders and pulled me closer. "Sebastian is my advisor. If our plans get out, it will put more lives as risk." He kissed my forehead. "You can talk to Sebastian too."

I laid my head in the hollow of his neck. "Couldn't we just talk to them?"

"I don't think that will work, princess."

I nodded against him. Part of me did understand, but the line was getting muddled and I couldn't tell which part was which anymore. "I won't mention your plans, but I still want to go. I need to think about everything with a clear head."

"And you don't have a clear head with me?"

"You could say I have trouble being objective around you, yeah . . ."

He laughed and kissed my hair. "I'm glad I am not the only one."

"But you'll take us to Chicago."

His chest rose against mine. "If that's what you want."

"So what do you want to do?" Sy asked, giving the stink eye to a burly, smelly bounty hunter who'd been leering at Kat and me since we got there.

"Talk to Jaron. Do you know how to reach him?"

He nodded. "He stopped by yesterday." He studied me for a moment. "You seem agitated. What happened? Something's changed." His eyes flickered between Katrina and me.

"She hasn't said a word since we left. I don't know." Kat sipped her cosmo.

"Nothing," I said into my glass. "I just need to make my decision sooner than later. If Michael is alive, he probably doesn't have a lot of time. Why haven't they contacted me? Where are the demands?"

Sy gave a helpless shrug. "I have no idea."

"That's why I need to talk to Jaron. I don't think Cheney's telling me everything about what happened pre-changeling. Maybe Jaron will."

"I'll get Jaron here, but I want to know what he says." Sy pulled out his phone, and with a few swift taps he proclaimed Jaron was on his way. "I'm helping you, Selene. Don't keep me in the dark."

Katrina shrugged. "She doesn't tell us anything either. She just told me about this Jaron person two days ago."

I rolled my eyes at them. "Speaking of Jaron, I don't want him to know who Katrina is, just in case." I looked at Sy and he frowned.

"As far as he's concerned, she'll be my guest."

Moments later Jaron walked through the door, filling the frame, shaking the rain out of his wavy hair. Katrina made a noise, but I ignored her. Out of the corner of my eye I saw Sy take her hand and stare into her eyes; she seemed to melt a little. I would've laughed if Jaron weren't headed directly for me.

"Take it to the back," Sy muttered. I nodded and led the big man to Sy's living room.

Jaron's presence filled the small area and saturated me. Everything about him was so familiar. It felt like if I looked at him long enough, everything would come back. I licked my lips. "Why did you follow me to the club?"

"I need you . . ." his jaw clenched, "to remember your obligations. If your plan has failed, it's time to start mine."

I reached up without thinking, about to run my hand along his tight jaw, but he dodged me. "How do you know I can't remember?"

His eyes flamed as he looked down. "Have a seat, Selene. It's going to be a long night."

"I'd rather stand." I had too much energy. I couldn't sit still.

"Do I make you nervous?" His voice was low and soft.

My heartbeat quickened, and a smug smile tilted his mouth. I mentally pushed back against his aura and squared my shoulders. He was not going to intimidate me. "Should I be?"

He raised a thick eyebrow. "Fear isn't weakness. Sometimes it's smart."

I narrowed my eyes. "I'm not afraid of you."

"Then you underestimate me." Something less than friendly glinted in his eyes. "Sit down. I may be helping you, but we're doing it on my terms this time. You need me more than I need you. Never forget that."

I sat and crossed my legs. He folded himself into the

armchair that almost was too small, his legs spread wide. "Did you enjoy your memory?"

My cheeks burned. I did enjoy the damn memory. It had felt real. I wasn't disconnected from myself in it. I could still feel his stubble scratching my face and the heat of his body. I shook off the thought and focused. "I'm with Cheney. Stop."

"Oh, I'm only just beginning." He folded his hands in his lap. "Would you like another one?"

I nodded, telling myself I was only interested to see if he could do it again.

"Come closer." I moved down the couch toward his chair until our knees were almost touching. He leaned forward and waited for me to do the same. I swallowed my worry and rested my elbows on my knees. I could feel the heat from his skin. He hooked a hand around the back of my neck and pulled me closer until our noses touched.

I pushed against his chest, breaking his hold. "What do you think you're doing?" My heart pounded and blood rushed through my veins. I couldn't want to kiss him, but I did. I was with Cheney. I ached for Cheney.

A languid smile spread over his lips. "These are your rules, not mine."

I shook my head. "What do you mean rules? You just touched my lips last time. No kissing was involved."

"You cast this spell. You set the parameters of it. I am just following them. If you want more than snippets, if you want your life back, you have no choice." He raised an eyebrow and waited.

I swallowed and chewed the inside of my cheek. I needed to remember. This wasn't cheating—it was what I had to do. I closed my eyes and nodded, as if not seeing myself give in would make it like it never happened.

"This isn't going to hurt." His velvet voice almost made me forget the ache in my chest and the worry in my stomach. His lips crushed into mine, igniting a fire inside of me that burned all thoughts away until one memory took center stage.

I finished putting the last ornament in the elaborate twists in the back of my hair—a perfect buttercup flower. I scoured every inch of myself for flaws. The soft lemon colored silk dress hung just right. The empire waist and capped sleeves were lined with a luscious chocolate satin. I pinched my cheeks and pressed my lips together hard to enhance the color. My dressing room door opened and Jaron walked through with long strides.

He kissed my cheek and stood behind me with his hands barely on my shoulders, looking at us in the mirror. He was always so careful when he touched me, like I might shatter into a million pieces. I didn't wait for a compliment—Jaron wasn't the type and that was one of my favorite things about him. Too many men wasted poems and sonnets on me. I didn't need pretty words; I needed strength and wisdom. Jaron had plenty of both. "Are you sure you want to do this?" he asked.

I flashed my most confident smile. "Perfectly."

Meeting my father for the first time was equal parts terrifying and thrilling. My human mother died with my birth, a far too common story amongst half-elves. Father did not want to raise a half-breed child, so he gave me to his exiled sister, Aunt Lorelei. She had fallen in love with a human, refused to give him up, and was exiled from the fae. She had a son near to me in age, Sy, and took me into her warm heart. Father never came to see us, even once.

"He's an important and influential man, Selene," she would tell me. "He has duties far greater than us."

But I was of age now, a woman by elven standards, and I intended to meet my father. The Erlking was hosting a feast in celebration of another successful hunt. Jaron procured us invitations; he was good at procuring things. And I was on a mission.

I walked into the glittering white castle, head high and eyes wide. I never dreamed of anything quite like this. It was utterly amazing. I glanced at Jaron and he didn't look impressed—he rarely ever was. Jaron was older than me, worldly, but we fit together perfectly from the first moment I met him. If I was a spider, he was my web. We skirted along the edges, listening for Father's name, Tahlik of Maern. When I was about to give up hope, Jaron pulled me to a stop and gave the smallest nod toward a man with smooth shimmering skin and eyes the color of melted gold. His nearly black hair was slicked back from his young face.

"How do you know that's him?" I whispered.

"I made a point to find out what he looked like before we came tonight," Jaron said.

I squeezed his arm. Then I released him and glided through the beautiful people to stop beside the man. He turned to me with a pleasant smile, but his face froze when he met my eyes. We stared at each other for what seemed like an eternity. His hand crept toward my face. "You look just like Elizabeth," he whispered.

"Hello, Father," I said just as quietly.

Tears filled his beguiling eyes—and mine.

"I—"

"Hello, Tahlik. Who do we have here?" a voice came from behind him.

My heart stopped. The Erlking. My head snapped toward the floor and I curtsied but never looked up. The Erlking didn't approve of mixing races, never had. I could feel his eyes on me, but I continued to study the marble floor.

"She's, well…" I watched my father's feet shift uncomfortably. "No one. She's nothing. A half-elf."

The king snapped his fingers. I wasn't certain what I should do. I began to explain and a hand took my arm. I looked back through the tears expecting to see Jaron, but two of the king's guards blocked my view.

"Father," I said. "If you would just talk to me—"

Neither the king nor my father acknowledged my words. The guards lifted me from the ground and carried me outside by my arms, tossing me unceremoniously into the night. I crumpled to the ground, ruining my new dress.

Strong arms lifted me up and crushed me in a hug. I sobbed on Jaron's shoulder and he held me tighter, but still so carefully. "I'm sorry, my love," he said, running a soothing hand over my back.

I opened my eyes, and Jaron sat back in his chair, watching me. I stayed in stunned silence. I did remember that. I never tried to speak to my father again after that night and he never contacted me. Jaron told me I didn't need a father. I had Aunt Lorelei, Sy, and him, but I was angry and I couldn't let it go. The anger built and built until I couldn't contain it anymore. That was when I started losing control and destroying anything in my wake.

"Your lips taste different," he said quietly.

"You've always been with me." I didn't comprehend his words. My mind was still spinning and blood was rushing through my veins as early memories poured back into me. It was like he broke the dam.

He looked down at his hands. "Why do you taste different, Selene?" The cold softness in his voice startled me back to reality. I tried to ignore the dizziness and talk to him.

"So this whole thing is about revenge because my father wouldn't accept me? Am I really that petty?"

Jaron grabbed my hand and squeezed it until I was worried he might crack the bones. I tried to pull away, but he held on. "This incident opened your eyes to the world we lived in. Half-elves—and any fae who stooped to associate with us—lived in fear and exile. We were barely tolerated as servants. You endeavored to change that. You made the Abyss take notice of us. We are not inferior. Your rebellion wasn't petty. It was revolutionary." Those smoldering eyes drilled into mine. "Now tell me. Why do you taste different?"

"I don't know what you mean."

He licked his lips and looked suspicious, but I had no idea why. Finally he dropped my hand.

"How did you give me that memory? Why didn't it hurt?"

Jaron's eye twitched and his fists were clenched, but his voice was calm. "All things in time."

"I need answers. Did you burn down my studio? Do you know where Michael is?"

He frowned. "I was only at your studio after it burned because I knew you would eventually come. I don't know who this Michael person is. Do you care to elaborate?"

"Michael was a human friend of mine, and he was

apparently taken. It wasn't by the rebels?"

A bitter laugh came from Jaron. "We would no sooner raise a finger against you than you would against your cousin."

I nodded.

He studied me for a long moment. "I can bring you back, Selene, but is that what you want?"

I bit my lip. I didn't know what I wanted anymore. "How do you have my memories?"

"You gave them to me. You were the changeling, and I was the key."

"You said I had a plan. What was it?"

"To win the prince and take the throne."

"How?"

"You have to kill him."

I nearly choked. "What's your plan?" I said between coughs.

"If you have become too attached to kill him, then I will do it for you. I'll finish what you started. Pull our race from the gutters."

I shook my head. "I can't let that happen."

He sneered. "Why am I not surprised? When I saw you with him at the coronation, looking at him so adoringly..." The knuckles on his fists turned white and he stood up so fast I jumped. "I have to go."

"Jaron..." He closed his eyes at the sound of his name, distracting me from whatever I was going to say. The fine lines at the corners begged to be traced, such a contrast to Cheney's flawless skin. The clenched muscles in his arms began to relax.

"Say my name again." The low rumble of his voice sent

chills down my spine.

I bit my lip, and my heart fluttered. "Jaron."

He grimaced and opened his eyes, all emotion gone. "Tomorrow, same time and place." He walked out without looking back.

I closed my eyes and leaned my head back on the couch.

"So?" Sy asked, appearing in the doorway with Kat looking over his shoulder.

"I'm more confused than ever." I looked over at them. "Is it possible I was in love with both of them?"

Sy thought about it for a moment. "Anything is possible, but I honestly never bought the idea you were in love with Cheney, no matter how much you paraded around with him. He stood for everything you were against your whole life. Jaron? Well, he was the perfect fit with the Selene I knew then."

SEVEN

Nothing was better for getting my mind off of everything than hanging out with my friends and pretending everything was normal. Katrina had somehow managed to get everyone to the castle again, and she swore she didn't tell them a thing about what was going on. She said Devin hadn't been sleeping. Her dreams had been strange and filled with blood, so all the girls had been on edge. We were in one of the more comfortable, less formal rooms in the castle, lounging around. I listened to them gab and tried not to think about why I hadn't heard anything from Femi, Baker, Olivia, or Holden. The wait was murder.

"Oh my gosh, Selene, you haven't told us about the vampires," Katrina said, clasping her hands in front of her. "Are they more *Fright Night* or *Vampire Diaries*? Not that it really matters. They're all hot."

"Neither, really. They seem like normal people. That probably makes them more dangerous because you forget they are dangerous." I stifled a yawn. I was exhausted. I spent the entire morning working on silently casting the transporting spell—a bit of elf magic that I couldn't seem to master. Swordplay came back to me easily, but the spells made me want to pull out my hair, go figure.

"Forget the vampires. You haven't told us why we're here." Jessica gave me a pointed look.

I was too tired to think of a lie. "Someone burned down my studio and kidnapped Michael—but there haven't been any ransom demands yet. I know people who are looking into it."

"What?" Devin moved to sit on the ottoman in front of me. "Are you okay, sweetie? You have to be going out of your mind."

"You felt off to me the moment you walked in the room. I thought you were just tired," Leslie said.

"I am tired. And worried." I rolled my neck. "But the people looking for him are really good at stuff like this. Now, I really don't want to think about it tonight."

Devin and Leslie gave me sympathetic smiles, but Katrina pulled through for me and changed the subject. "In more important news, I got to hang out with Selene's hot cousin—and I've been meaning to ask you . . . Is he looking for a human girlfriend?"

I laughed. "I've never known Sy to turn down a pretty girl."

"Says the girl with no memory," Jessica said with a smile.

It occurred to me suddenly that she was wrong. I *did* remember. The memory sparked by Jaron's kiss brought back my entire youth up to the point of the memory. I couldn't say with certainty that Sy hadn't changed, but picturing his cheerful, lopsided smile, I had doubts.

"You remember, don't you?" Leslie said.

"How much? What was being an elf like? Tell us everything about your life," Devin said in an excited ramble as she leaned forward with her elbows on her knees.

"Why don't we let Selene breathe, Dev?" Jess said. "I think she just wants to take her mind off things."

"Exactly," I said.

"We can do that," Leslie said.

We spent the rest of the afternoon laughing and talking about our lives before everything went weird and people wanted to kill me and kidnap my friends. Before too long, it was time to go back to Sy's, and I hadn't even told Cheney I was going out again. I said goodbye to my friends, who decided to stay and hang out with Kat, before going to find Cheney. I heard his muffled voice down the hallway.

"I really don't think now is the right time for that. Shouldn't we wait until everything is in order?" Cheney said.

"No. The people need to see the two of you together. Right now they only know that you said you are married to Selene. If you have a public renewal of vows, it will remove any doubt."

I stopped and listened.

"I don't know that Selene is ready. We have put a lot on her shoulders, and she's still trying to remember everything."

"Exactly." There was a pause, and I didn't follow Sebastian's meaning. "Cheney, Selene made an excellent point when she said she might never remember. I have no idea why her memories are gone but they are and I know I don't need to remind you—"

"No," Cheney's voice was low and dark.

"She can't even perform elf magic. I don't know that she will ever be the Selene she was, and you should be grateful for that. She is much improved."

I rapped on the door before Cheney could respond. I

didn't want to hear what he thought about that that. I was a chicken. I stuck my head in the room. "I'm going to hang out with Sy again tonight. The girls are going to stick around here."

Cheney froze mid-smile. "You've been spending a lot of time with him."

I laughed. "You can't possibly be jealous of my cousin. He's telling me about our childhoods. I think it's helping me. Besides, you and Sebastian are so busy."

Cheney stood. "I guess you need me to take you."

"Actually, Sy's picking me up." I kissed his cheek. "Don't wait up." With that, I got the hell out of there before he could propose. I ignored the ache at being parted from him so quickly. It was better than being forced to make a new commitment to a man I wasn't sure I should be committed to in the first place.

Sy stood in the great hall, waiting for me with an amused expression. "I'll never get used to you living here."

"You'd rather I live in a seedy bar?"

"Hey, it's not seedy. It's..."

"Vile?"

"Lived in," he said with a firm nod that made me laugh.

How was it that Sy managed to grow up in the same world as me and not be turned bitter by it? He transported us back to Chicago. "Why is it that you don't mind how half-elves are treated?"

He paused, hand on the door to his pub. "I didn't wait for anyone to give me what I wanted. I made my life what it is and have earned the respect of those who work with me. However, I work with the Abyss at large, not just the fae. You never could see that there was a much larger world out there than the small one that wouldn't accept you."

I felt a bit stung by his words, though I knew that wasn't his intention, and he gave me a curious look before holding the door open for me. Jaron was already waiting inside.

Jaron gave Sy a small nod and followed me back to his living room.

"You're late," he said.

"I lost track of—"

"If it happens again, I'll end this arrangement. I won't come second to him."

I closed my eyes and bit back a snarky retort. Jaron had the manners of an invading horde, but I needed him. He had my memories. "Then let's not waste anymore time."

He raised an eyebrow and pulled a container of breath spray out of the air. He did two squirts then offered it to me with a wink. I reached out to take it, but he caught my hand and pulled me toward him. His hand splayed against the small of my back, yet he barely touched me. My heart sped in my chest and my lungs constricted. He leaned down, his mouth almost to mine.

"Why hadn't you met Sy before now?" I asked, stalling while a new rush of nerves washed over me. If kissing Jaron meant nothing to me, it would've been easier. I wouldn't feel like I was hurting Cheney—but it did mean something and that scared the crap out of me.

Jaron paused, his eyes meeting mine for just a moment, then he closed the rest of the distance between us. His lips gently brushed against mine, making my head lull back. I curled my fingers into his blue button down shirt, fighting the urge to push him away. I could feel a memory bearing down on me, but it wasn't quite there. A need to know what it was overcame my reservations. I broke the kiss but kept ahold of his shirt and dragged him to the small counter that divided Sy's miniscule kitchen from his living room. I nudged Jaron. "Up."

His hands encased my hips and he lifted me up, setting me on top of the counter. I kissed him this time, harder, winding my fingers into his soft waves and pulling his face closer. A mewling sound formed in the back of my throat and his tongue slipped in, stroking mine. With the motion, everything drifted away.

I was lying in bed next to Cheney, listening to his even breath. What the hell was I doing here? I glanced at the clock. It was almost time. A rush of adrenaline coursed through my veins as I slipped from between the covers and silently moved out the door. I lightly ran down the stairs out front, ignoring the chill of the night air biting my skin. My thin, champagne colored silk nightgown did little to cover me, but I didn't care. It had been months since the last time Jaron agreed to see me. I wove through the trees, deeper and deeper into the forest, until I found him waiting for me.

"You're late," he growled.

"But I'm worth the wait." I wrapped my arms around him, burying my face in his hard chest, inhaling his scent.

He brushed my hands away and cold air assaulted me once more. "I warned you, Selene, before you left."

"Yet, here you are." I gave him my most dazzling smile. "Now stop complaining and keep me warm while we talk."

He frowned and shrugged his jacket off, handing it to me. It was a poor substitution, but I took it. "What do you want?"

"I figured out how expedite this entire process." I waited for him to react.

He sighed. "I'm listening."

"I'll become a changeling." I bit my lip in excitement. "It's brilliant, isn't it? I'll get away from Cheney and come back twice as powerful. It will work. We can do it."

Jaron crossed his arms and looked down at me. "What makes you think so?"

"My mother was a human witch. If I do this, the fae will have no control over me. I'll be free."

"Freedom is an illusion. It won't change anything. You've spent all this time winning the prince over and now you almost have him where we need him. Why stop?" His eyes were dark and unreadable.

"I'm not stopping. I'm strengthening the plan. Cheney is strong. I don't know if I can do what we talked about. I need more power."

Jaron raised his eyebrows. "But you'll kill him once you're in a position of power."

"If it comes to that."

Jaron's eyes iced over. "You have feelings for him, don't you?"

I studied the ground as I thought about how to explain my feelings to him. "If I don't have to, I don't want to hurt him. Maybe we can do this peacefully."

"Or maybe we should break off from the fae and form our own society, like I've been saying. Look what your cousin has managed to do."

"I'm a half-elf. I have every right to be here. The king is wrong. His policy is wrong. And I'm going to set it right if it's the last thing I do." I wove my magic around him as I spoke, rendering him unable to move. He hated it when I did that, which was exactly why I chose this particular method to make him listen. "It will work. This is what you trained me for."

Plucking his very thin string of control was probably a bad idea, but I didn't care. Jaron taught me how to control my feelings and to play the game the fae called life. I was tired of him being in control. I wanted him to feel helpless like us lesser mortals. Maybe then he would run wild and free with me. It was a risk, but the payoff would be limitless.

"Don't push me." His voice was soft and thin.

I tightened my hold. My control of him broke with nearly an audible snap. He lifted me off the ground, his fingers digging into my arms. "Do. Not. Push. Me. Selene." His breath was ragged.

"Live, Jaron. Let go. Why do you always hold back? What's so great about being in control?"

He dropped me to the ground and backed away, staring at the red blotches on my arms. "Leave, Selene. Don't come back."

Jaron's head was on my shoulder, and I was slumped against him when I came back. Not sure what to say, I ran my fingers through his hair instead of speaking.

"I was goading you on purpose. I wanted you to lose control."

His chest rose with his breath, and a moment later he straightened. "I can't lose control. You don't understand."

There he was wrong. I did understand now. Better than anyone maybe. Thanks to my telekinetic abilities, when I got emotional and lost control, I destroyed everything around me.

I wasn't sure what happened when Jaron lost control, but no one who held on that tightly did so without reason. "Actually, I think I do." I offered him my hand, letting touching me be his decision.

He looked at my hand as if it were on fire.

"So that whole thing about breaking off from the elves, is that still possible?" I asked.

Jaron tore his eyes from my hand. "Are you serious?"

I thought about what Sebastian and Cheney had discussed. I didn't want there to be a war. If the half-elves left, Cheney could claim he exiled them and save face. We could leave. . . . No, I shook my head slightly. I couldn't leave. I rubbed the spot on my chest where the bond ached and felt like crying, though it had nothing to do with the pain. "Maybe."

Jaron touched my face, as if seeing me for the first time. "This isn't what you want."

If the half-elves exiled themselves, what would that mean for me? Would I never see Sy or Jaron again? If I kept playing both sides, how long would it be before I tripped up and this house of cards crumbled? Would Cheney change his mind if he knew everything? Would he still love me? "You don't need me to do it."

Jaron's face snapped closed, and his hand dropped to his side.

I looked down. "I no longer care about being an elf." My words were true. I didn't care. I couldn't tell if my elf half cared anymore or if she'd given up. There was only one thing that was clear to me. It was time to talk to Cheney.

EIGHT

Sy took me back to the castle. It was late, and everything was quiet and serene. It somehow looked different now, tainted by my memory. I walked slowly through the great hall, reliving the memory of meeting my father, expecting the guards to rush in and carry me away again. With each memory Jaron gave me, I felt a little closer to my past self, which was beyond frightening. The memories I got on my own seemed forced, like I was ripping them from my mind. The ones Jaron gave felt organic. I didn't just remember the one feeble scene; all of my life surrounding the event became clear. And now I could clearly see I'd put myself in quite the predicament. My intentions were good originally, but I took them too far. I couldn't believe I had ever considered killing Cheney. I guessed I was trying to make decisions like an elf and ignore my feelings. Why had I agreed to be bonded to Cheney, and why did I give Jaron my memories?

Sy's voice rang through my thoughts. I needed to figure out what I wanted *now*, regardless of how I felt then. I couldn't let myself get wrapped up in the memories.

"I thought you'd be later," Cheney said from the doorway.

I looked up and smiled at him, still rooted to the spot

where I'd spoken with my father, though Cheney pulled at me like a magnet. "I was ready to come home."

"I'm glad." Cheney walked toward me with graceful, light steps. He was so different than Jaron. His thinner, rangy body coated with lean muscles seemed frail compared to Jaron's taller, thicker build. Cheney's face was smooth and timeless, and Jaron's was weathered and rugged. His hair was wild and impish, whereas Jaron's was wavy and relaxed. How did I manage to love two such different men? Then again, maybe I never loved Cheney at all. Maybe I just fooled both of us.

Cheney's arms curled around me, and he feathered kisses along the side of my neck. "What are you doing in here?"

I bent my head to the side to give him better access and sighed. "Do you think my father is still alive?"

Cheney froze. "Have you remembered something?"

I almost told him my memory, but something inside stopped me. "Why do you ask? Does it matter if I remember something? Would it change your answer?"

His embrace tightened. "He is still alive, yes."

"Why didn't you tell me?"

"You never wanted to discuss your family—any of them. I'm actually surprised you're so close to Sy now. Do you want to meet him? I can summon him to the court."

"No," I said softly, remembering our last meeting with a heavy heart. I didn't dislike my elf side anymore. For better or worse, I understood her now—at least a little. "We don't need any more complications."

He smoothed my hair from my face and resumed kissing my neck. "If it makes you happy…"

"Finding Michael alive and well and putting an end to all of this fighting would accomplish that."

His tongue traced my pulse. "Has Sy made any progress?"

"Mmm." His hands grazed down my sides as he pulled my earlobe into his mouth. Elves have highly sensitive ears, and with enough pressure in the right spot, I could shatter into a million pieces. His tongue ran along the edge and my knees shook. I leaned into him for support.

"Did I mention that I'm glad you came home?" He chuckled softly, his breath cooling the spots he'd just set to fire. "Let's go back to our room."

I pulled away, shaking my head with a teasing smile. "I'm happy where I am." I took his hand and led him toward the front of the room. "Are you worried someone will catch us?"

He laughed. "Not at all."

I pushed him into the throne, straddling his legs. "There's something I need to talk to you about." I kissed him softly but couldn't stop comparing him to Jaron.

"Is it urgent?" He tugged my shirt over my head, pulling a nipple into his mouth.

"God, yes." He paused and my breath caught. "Don't stop."

He chuckled and resumed the motion.

Talking could wait until morning.

Cheney and I made it down to the gym before Sebastian

for once, and while we waited, Cheney kissed the back of my hand, his eyes twinkling. "There are 283 rooms in this castle. Do you think we should christen them all?"

I laughed. "We certainly could try." I still wasn't sure what I needed to do. This connection with Cheney was impossible to ignore, and it was impossible to think objectively when I was here. When I was with him all I wanted was more, but when we were apart I was riddled with doubt. There had to be a way to break the bond. It was the only way I would ever know what I actually felt.

"There was something you wanted to talk to me about?"

My hands went instantly cold and I pulled away from him. "Sit down, Cheney."

He gave me a strange look but took his seat. "You did remember something, didn't you?"

I paced away, not sure how to do this. "I know who the leader of the rebels is." His eyebrows shot up and he started to stand, but I waved him back down. I licked my dry lips. "Apparently it's me."

"That's absurd. You don't know what you're talking about. You can't remember. You're not their leader."

"Femi did some checking into the rebels and brought the current leader to me. He doesn't want to kill me, Cheney. We don't understand the rebels as well as we thought. He said I was their leader. I started the movement with him. The whole thing was a setup from the start with you."

The blood drained from Cheney's face and his hands pressed into his knees. "How long have you known?"

My heart thumped in my chest and my throat tightened. "Not long." My eyes drifted to the floor.

His hands were on my shoulders in a second, fingers

digging in my flesh, but not enough to hurt. He shook me slightly. "How long?" The words were a growl.

I met his molten gold eyes. "I found out right after you took the crown."

He released me so fast I stumbled. He backed away and ran his hand through his hair. "Convenient. No wonder you don't want the rebels punished." He stared at me. "You've played me from the start, haven't you? Did you even lose your memory?"

"You know I lost my memory. Sy and I have been trying to figure out exactly what she was up to, but so far we haven't gotten far."

"Damn it, Selene, you are not two people." He whirled around on me. "Do you think your lack of a memory coincides with your lack of wanting to take responsibility for your actions? Have you been seeing him, whoever this mysterious partner in crime is?"

Anger and hurt mixed with my guilt. If he wanted me to be responsible for what she did, then fine, I would be responsible for it, but I wasn't turning over Jaron. I'd done enough harm to him. I nodded and took a step toward Cheney, though my heart cracked and bled at the sight of his anguish. Tears filled my eyes. "I'm sorry I couldn't love you like you loved me."

"Don't." He held up his hand and walked away.

I closed my eyes against the pain in my chest. "I would never have hurt you," I whispered as the door closed behind him and I crumpled to the floor. I curled into a fetal position and lay on cold stone ground as tears seeped from my shut eyes. It wasn't fair. None of this was fair.

I don't know how long I stayed like that. The thought

that my reaction wasn't behavior becoming of a leader found its way into my mind. I took several deep breaths and forced my eyes open. Then I pushed myself off the floor with shaking hands, straightening my shoulders. I wasn't going to solve anything while lying on the floor. Sy and I would get to the bottom of this and I would make everything right. I started for the door when it opened. Sebastian came through, glancing around.

"Where's Cheney?"

I couldn't answer him, the words stuck in my throat, so I continued past him. He took my arm. "Selene?"

I looked back, knowing my eyes had to be red and swollen.

Sebastian frowned but didn't let go. "Where are you going?"

"Stay out of this, Sebastian."

He stared at me for a moment before releasing me. I started for the door again. "The old you runs away, Selene. Find him and talk to him. Don't make him come after you again."

"He doesn't want to talk to me." My voice was scratchy and raw.

"Cheney always forgives you," Sebastian said quietly.

I headed toward our bedroom to pack, taking a different route than usual, hoping to avoid seeing anyone. I paused at a heavy wooden door. It was familiar and something in me knew who I would find on the other side. My trembling fingers pressed the cool polished wood. Holding my breath, I turned the handle and entered.

Cheney sat low in a chair, his legs sprawled out in front of him, with a glass of dark amber liquid in his hand. He didn't look up at me, but he stiffened and took a drink. I closed the door silently and sat in the chair across from him, letting the stillness linger.

"How many rooms did you check before you found me?" His voice was tired and low.

I swallowed and wiped another stray tear from my eye. "This was the first."

He gave a bitter half-laugh and took another drink. "You remember quite a lot when you want to."

I clenched my jaw but didn't say anything. I honestly didn't know if I'd ever even been here before. Given his father, I expected not. I got up and retrieved a glass to pour myself a drink from the decanter on the table next to him. I refilled his glass too. Cheney stared straight ahead. I resumed my seat in his line of sight.

"You made a fool out of me."

I closed my eyes and took a drink. It tasted like nothing I'd ever had before—a cross between Everclear and honey that scalded my throat and chest as it slid down to my stomach. I sat the offending glass to the side.

"I'm sorry," I said. It was the only thing I could think to say.

"We're so far beyond apologies. Do you love him?"

"I think I did at the time."

Cheney took another drink. "I gave up everything for you. I went against my family, my kind. I invited other races in, all to make you happy."

I shook my head. "What you're doing is bigger than us. It's important to unite. Things can't continue as they are."

"How do you know?" he yelled and chucked his glass across the room. "You've gotten everything you wanted. You destroyed my family. You humiliated me. You brought my race to its knees, and all the while I've been praising you. Thinking how strong you were to stand against your own kind."

He didn't want excuses and I didn't have explanations. "What do you want me to do?"

He shook his head. "Just leave."

I nodded and stood. "The room or the palace?" I held my breath as I waited for his reply.

Cheney turned his head away from me. "I don't care."

The last of my hope died with his words. I retreated.

"Did you ever love me, Selene?" his broken voice asked as my hand touched the door handle.

I couldn't bring myself to turn back to him. "I don't know if I did then, but I thought I might now." The back of my throat burned. "For the record, I'm not the one running this time."

I slipped through the door and found my way to our room through watery vision. I tossed clothes, make up, and my cell phone charger into a duffle bag. Then, sniffling, I pulled my cell phone from my pocket and texted Sy. I braced my arms against the bed, waiting for his reply. I'd made the right decision. I had to tell Cheney. It wasn't fair to keep it a secret.

"Don't leave." Sebastian's voice made me look up.

"He told me to." I went to the closet and got more clothing so I didn't have to look in his sympathetic eyes.

"He didn't mean it."

"Sebastian—"

"No. For once be quiet and listen. I have stood by for too long and watched you make a mess of this. Cheney is perfect for you and you are perfect for him. He would and has done everything for you. Just let yourself feel something for him. Stop thinking so much."

"You don't understand. I'm going to keep hurting him until I figure this out. This is for the best. I'm taking responsibilities for actions."

"You don't have to do it alone."

"I will fix it. I swear." I wiped away a stray tear. "Maybe it won't be too late and he'll still want me when the dust settles."

"He loves you now."

"He doesn't know me. I don't even know myself." I hugged Sebastian tight. "Take care of him." I slung my bag over my shoulder and went for the door.

"You can't leave," Sebastian said.

"Why not?"

"Because no matter what happened between the two of you, if you leave now, the movement you started will shatter. At the very least, you two have to keep up appearances."

"What does that mean?"

"It means regardless of where you stay the night, you have to be here during the day."

"And Cheney will be okay with that?"

He nodded. "He knows what's at stake."

"Fine. Katrina and I will be back in the morning if you do something for me."

"What?"

"Find a way to break our bond."

Sebastian stared at me for a long time with calculating eyes. "I will look into it. Don't give up, Selene."

"I'm not giving up. I'm looking for what's real."

NINE

I hadn't seen more than Sy's living room and small kitchen. In fact, I couldn't swear there was more than a living room. "Are you sure you don't mind us staying with you?"

"I'm glad to have you guys here." He slung one arm around my shoulder and one around Katrina's. "I could use some extra help around the bar. I'll teach you guys the business." He went back behind the counter.

I laughed and shook my head, flopping down on a stool. "How do you like the new place?" I asked Katrina, my eyes filling with tears again. "What am I going to do?" I laid my head in my arms.

Kat patted my shoulder.

"Well, first, stop crying. What kind of elf goes around crying all the time? Pull yourself together," Sy said, sliding me a drink. "Second, find yourself an occupation, like, say, bartending. Have I mentioned I could use the help? And if you could break up fights between wound up bounty hunters so your dear old cousin could take a night off . . . Well, that'd be perfect."

"I used to tend bar in college. I'm your girl," Katrina told him.

"You bet you are." Sy winked.

I groaned. "Fine. Teach me what you can before Jaron gets here. We have to go back to the castle during the day. Keeping up appearances." I rolled my eyes.

Sy patted my arm. "I'm going to have to hire bouncers with the two of you in this bar."

I ran my fingers through my hair, trying to convince myself we'd be fine. "Have you heard from Femi? Any news?"

"She should be around soon. She said something about bringing Olivia and Holden, too." A worried line creased his forehead. "You know who would really like to see you again? Mom."

"Aunt Lorelei?"

Sy grinned. "You remember!"

Katrina had turned around in her seat to inspect the tables of bounty hunters, though I could tell she was still listening to us.

"Yeah, I had a memory the other night about my father. I think I remember everything before that now. I remember Aunt Lorelei smelling like cinnamon and vanilla. I remember my bedroom was a deep royal blue. I remember us fighting and playing hide-and-go-seek."

"I didn't know you met your father." Sy leaned on his forearms against the counter. "What happened?"

As I told him, he looked at me with sad eyes.

"I'm sorry, sweetie," Kat said, no longer interested in our surroundings, but it was Sy's stare that began to crack my emotional walls. I looked away. I couldn't take it. I understood why I stayed away from Sy and Aunt Lorelei before. I loved them both too much. I felt safe with them and that made me let down my guard. They loved me just for me, unconditionally, and I couldn't bear the idea of them being hurt. I forced a smile and changed the subject. "So what's the deal with you and Femi?"

Katrina took my cue. "Femi?"

Sy smiled. Not his typical confident, charming grin, but a sweet, dreamy tilt to his lips. "She's great, isn't she?"

I nodded. "Are you two …" I raised my eyebrows.

He rolled his neck. "Our world is complicated. Sometimes things just don't work out."

I shrugged. "Seems like you're giving up pretty easily to me."

The door opened and Olivia and Holden walked in. "Who said I was giving up?" Sy said.

"Whoa," Katrina breathed.

"Hi." Olivia smiled and waved, radiant as ever. Holden's eyes scanned the room, calculating threats. "Are you okay?" she asked when she got closer.

I bit my lip and nodded.

"Hi, I'm Liv and this is Holden," she said to Katrina.

"Katrina. I'm Selene's friend."

"It's nice to meet you." Olivia looked back at me. "No offense, but there's something off about you today." She motioned her hand vaguely around me.

"She left Cheney," Sy told them and I gave him a look. He made a face at me.

"They're bonded magically, so though she's hiding it, she's hurting," Kat said, ignoring me.

I rolled my eyes. "Neither the bond nor my leaving is public knowledge. You two obviously can't keep secrets."

Holden gave me a withering look. "I don't think Liv or I know anyone who would care."

Olivia shook her head. "No, I think what Holden means is we're sorry you're in pain."

Holden didn't look like he meant that at all. I laughed. "Actually I appreciate his candor. Reminds me of my coven."

"Well, your secret is safe with us." Olivia smiled sadly, studying the area around me. "I might be able to do something. Do you mind?" she asked, her hand hovering over me. I shook my head. She pressed her palm flat against my chest, just above where it hurt, and a lovely white light poured from her and blanketed me. Katrina gasped and started whispering furiously to Sy. Any remaining tears dried and my mind eased, but her effort did nothing to help with the deep festering pain.

Olivia frowned. "Hmmm. I don't have any experience with magical bonds." She looked over her shoulder at Holden. "What do you think?"

Holden came up behind her and looked at her hand just above my breasts. "What exactly do you have in mind, Liv?" A slight smile ticked his lips.

Olivia rolled her eyes and stayed focused on me. "He can manipulate emotion—I can't. If your bond is emotionally based, he might be able to tweak it. It wouldn't be a permanent fix, but it could help." She looked back at him. "You can do that, right?"

Holden's face turned serious as he studied me with a detachment that made me want to squirm.

"I feel a lot calmer now. That's enough. I can deal with this. Thank you," I told her and she released me.

Holden sat down on the stool beside me. "I might be able to do something. I know nothing about magic, but emotions are emotions and yours are running high. But this isn't a decision you should make lightly. You need to be sure you want me to meddle with your feelings."

My stomach twisted, and I fought against the nerves. "What exactly would you do?"

The door slammed against the wall. "I love the smell of stale beer in the morning," Femi proclaimed loudly. "So team, what do we know?"

"Just a sec, we're fixing Selene," Sy said, winking at Femi.

"Is she broken?" Femi walked up and stood next to Olivia while Holden inspected me again. "What's wrong with you, Hermione?"

"Nothing." I crossed my arms over my chest. I tried to ease the irritation boiling up inside me—these people were helping me—but it simmered and popped inside of me. "I just need to figure out how to break this stupid bond."

"Who brought the human?" she asked.

"This is Katrina. She's in my coven."

Femi tilted her head and eyed Katrina. "You're in my seat."

Katrina shifted. "I guess you'll have to find a new one."

Femi smiled. "You might be all right." She looked back to me. "Why do you want to break the bond?"

I gave a quick rundown of the fight Cheney and I had, and Holden scoffed. "We told you to keep doing what you were doing, not confess everything you know. Did you even find out where they're holding his father?"

"No, I didn't have chance. And I didn't tell him everything, but I had to tell him this. I didn't mention Jaron by name, but I did tell him that the rebels aren't responsible for my studio or Michael. You don't understand. He hates them and blames them for everything. Cheney would have come after them and I could prevent it. I saved lives."

"So the human's life is worth preventing an attack that may never have happened?" he asked.

I ground my teeth together, stunned. I hadn't even considered the danger I'd put Michael in. Why hadn't I thought things through better?

Holden continued on in a flat, emotionless voice. "If Cheney's responsible for Michael's abduction, he now knows you don't believe his story. That makes the human worthless unless Cheney confesses his involvement and holds his life over your head for cooperation." Holden gave me a cold glare. "Did you want the human to die? If so, why are you wasting my time? I have other matters to take care of."

I looked over at Katrina, who was staring at her feet with a contemplative expression.

"Hey," Sy said. "She's had a rough morning. Don't be a dick."

"We all make questionable decisions when it comes to the heart," Olivia said, raising an eyebrow. "Even you." Holden looked at her and nodded.

"Sorry," he told me in a stiff way that made me think he didn't apologize often.

I didn't want his apology. If he was right, then I'd royally messed up and needed to hear what he had to say. I let my past confuse my present and I'd made another bad decision. "Don't apologize. You're right."

"So what have you found out?" Femi asked, and I was grateful for the subject change.

"There wasn't much at the studio. But we did find this at your house." Holden produced a letter and handed it to me.

"Basically it says blah, blah, blah, do what we want or we kill the human."

"What do they want?" My hands shook too badly to read the letter. Sy took the paper from me, studying it. "Who sent it? How long has it been there?"

"There was nothing at your house the night I called you," Femi said. "Jaron has been hard to follow with all the transporting shit you people do, but as far as I can tell, he goes to one of three places: here, his home, and a church."

"What church?" I asked.

Femi shrugged. "I think it's where the rebels meet, but I could be wrong. I haven't gone inside yet. What does the letter say?"

"They want her to give Jaron to Cheney for a public execution as punishment for leading the rebellion."

It didn't help me trust Cheney more that the note's demands worked in his favor. It mirrored his plan for defeating the rebels a little too closely to be a coincidence. "Does the note ask for him by name?" I asked.

Olivia shook her head.

Did Cheney know about my involvement before I told him? Did he think I confessed to starting the rebellion to save Jaron? I tugged at my lip, not wanting to believe what my mind was thinking. If it wasn't Cheney, then perhaps the letter wasn't referring to Jaron at all. Perhaps the letter was meant to get me to expose myself. "I'm not killing anyone on either side. Has Baker found out anything about Alanna?"

Holden shook his head. "Not yet. Who else are you supposed to kill?"

"Jaron wants me to kill Cheney and take the throne."

"Huh," Sy said. "So they both want you to kill the other

one."

I shook my head. "Cheney never asked me to kill anyone."

"Unless he wrote this letter," Holden said.

"So you're definitely thinking Cheney is behind all of this?" My head immediately shook. "It isn't possible. That isn't who he is."

"We don't have enough information to make judgments," Holden said. "Right now we're just working out the possibilities."

"What about you, lover? Have you found us any more suspects?" Femi asked Sy.

"Actually, no. Elves aside, the rest of the fae seem to like Selene more than they like Cheney. I'm actually surprised he let you leave him."

I resisted the urge to lay my head down. "He couldn't even look at me when I left. Sebastian is the one who told me I still have to perform my queenly obligations. Whatever the hell that means."

Holden rubbed his jaw. "It means you need to be careful. Cheney might have let you go so he can keeps tabs on you and on who you're meeting now that he knows you don't blindly trust him. Making you keep up appearances leaves him as a hero in the public eye. He still has all the appearance of forward thinking while gaining information on his enemies. It's actually an elegant plan. He gets public sympathy, the appearance of good will, and the traitor exposed all without lifting a blade or spilling a drop of his people's blood." He cracked his knuckles. "Jaron should watch his back if he's going to keep meeting with you."

"He's supposed to come here tonight. I'll warn him," I

said.

"I found something else." Olivia grimaced and looked away as Holden pulled a severed finger in a plastic baggie from his jacket pocket.

"You cut off someone's finger?" Katrina squeaked.

"Not recently." Holden winked at her and tossed the bag onto the bar. I glanced over at Katrina. She was staring at Holden with a slightly dreamy expression. "I'd be willing to bet it's the human's."

"That's ... oh, God." I couldn't look away. Once I swallowed down my revulsion, I had an idea. "I can find Michael with that." I reached for the bag, but Sy pulled it away from me.

"What if they know that? If all of this is a trap to draw you out? Burning down the studio got you out of the castle, and now a finger any witch could use to cast a tracking spell. It seems too convenient."

I snatched the bag from him. "I'm not going to let them kill him because he had the bad fortune to think he was in love with me," I snapped.

"You're not running head first into traps." Sy plucked the baggie back from my fingers. "I'll put this on ice until we're ready for it."

"Why are we waiting?" I demanded. We finally had a lead.

"We need information," Femi said. "If we charge in there now, we might save him and learn nothing. Then we'll have to start from the beginning when your next friend is kidnapped. You've already tilted our hand to Cheney enough. Until we have a pretty good idea that Michael is in real danger or who is behind this and what they want, we aren't doing anything."

"Did they give a deadline?" I asked Holden.

He folded his arms behind his back. "No. They also didn't give a way to reach them."

"So they want a public display," Femi said.

"But what if Cheney isn't involved? Maybe he would help us fake an execution. That way he would have his justice in the public eye and whoever is doing this would release Michael."

"That's putting an awful lot of faith in two people you don't trust," Olivia said softly.

"I hate doing nothing," I said, matching her tone.

"You aren't doing nothing. You still have access to the castle. You're our eyes and ears inside," Femi told me.

"We could help too," Katrina said and charged on before I could object. "Sy's place really isn't big enough for both of us. I can talk to the other girls and get them all to move into the castle with me. Cheney would have to let us stay because if you have to keep up appearances, so does he. With four of us snooping around the castle, surely we can discover something."

"I don't know—"

"Sebastian might be willing to talk to me, too."

"Are you sure you want to do this?" Sy asked.

I didn't like the idea of them snooping around, but Katrina was probably right that they'd be good at it. "What about breaking the bond? Can we do that?"

"We don't know that you need to. He might be innocent," Olivia said.

"Even if he is, I want it broken. I need space. I need to figure out what I want and how I feel without being magically influenced."

"Okay, we'll get back together in a couple days." Femi went to the bar to talk to Sy and Katrina. Olivia and Holden, judging by their distant expressions, were talking silently with one another. I was alone with my thoughts and the pain in my chest from missing Cheney.

"I'm going to go lie down. I have a headache," I told Sy and headed for the back.

Holden caught my arm and pulled me over to him and Olivia. "I might be able to redirect your feelings. It would be a very temporary fix, definitely not a solution. And it could backfire. Magical bonds are a pain in the ass."

"I don't think you should break it. If Holden can ease the effects so you can wait this out, that's what I recommend," Olivia said. "Let Holden try."

Holden frowned at her. "I might not be able to do anything. I told you this isn't the same as that. You're thinking with your heart. Magic has nothing to do with souls. You and I are bonded on a molecular level; she is bonded by a spell. It's more like the arrangements the jinn have with demons. But instead of having her soul, Cheney has her life. If she dies, he dies and vice versa. That's why no one gets married in the Abyss."

My eyebrows shot up. No one had explained this to me before. "So that's why he came to help me when the bounty hunters were after me? If I die, he dies."

Holden nodded. "Probably. Breaking this bond might actually fix a lot of your immediate problems."

"You don't know that," Olivia argued, frowning right back at him. "If they love each other, Holden, why break them up."

"Who says they're in love?" he shot back. "Not everyone thinks with their heart."

I looked back and forth between the two of them. How on earth did they ever end up together? "Why would he bond himself to me? I won't live as long as him."

"Exactly," Olivia said with a triumphant smile.

Holden rolled his eyes. "You will so long as you're bonded."

Again, that was news to me. "And had I decided to stay a human?"

"Cheney would have a very short life expectancy."

I shook my head. I had a lot to consider. "I'm going to tough this out until I can break the bond, but thank you for your offer to help." I looked at Olivia. "The problem I have is the more I remember, the more I doubt I ever loved Cheney. I don't know if the pull I feel toward him is my true feelings or the side effect of whatever plan I had. And I don't want to decide the rest of my life based on manufactured feelings. And then there's Jaron." I looked toward the door. "I'm not indifferent to him."

Olivia smiled. "That's very logical." She looked at Holden out of the corner of her eye and placed a gentle hand on my arm. "But love isn't logical. Even the strongest magic can't make your heart lie. Only you can know what you truly feel." She released me and took Holden's hand. He kissed the back of hers.

"If you change your mind …" he said absently, no longer interested in me as he watched Olivia glow.

I went back into Sy's apartment and lay on the couch. All I had to do was break an impossible bond, steal Michael's finger back, save him, and swear off men for the rest of my life and the world would be perfect.

"That was the craziest meeting I've ever been to." Katrina plopped down by my feet. "Femi is sort of hilarious. What the hell happened when you and Olivia disappeared?"

"What? I didn't disappear."

"You did too. She put her hand on you and poof you were both gone."

"They weren't gone," Sy said from the doorway. "Olivia is a guardian. She was healing Selene. That generally makes them invisible to mortals."

"Oh, and Holden. Is he a guardian too?"

Sy laughed. "Are you okay, coz?"

"I'm great," I mumbled. "Can you cancel my meeting with Jaron tonight? I'm not up for another memory. I already have too much to think about."

"Sure. If you need anything, let me know."

I sat up. "Are you really going back to castle?"

"It's already arranged. I spoke with Sebastian and the girls. Selene, I want to help. We all want to help. We'll be fine and figure all of this out. Besides, I don't think Cheney's guilty. I like him and I like the way you are when you're with him—less cautious and more alive. I think the two of you will work things out."

"I hope you're right."

"Now I say we get some ice cream and wine and watch chick flicks."

It was hard to argue with such a solid plan.

TEN

I walked into the gym right on time but with heavy circles under my eyes. Sleep was a fickle lover, taunting me, but never taking me all night long. And while I'd tossed and turned, a new question had assailed me. Why hadn't the bond affected me before I knew about it? Sebastian looked up and gave his typical greeting. After I sat, he said, "So are you going to tell me the details?"

I shrugged.

Sebastian raised an eyebrow. "One of you has to. Cheney won't say anything, but he paced the hallways all night. All Katrina said was that you'd be staying with Sy for a while—wouldn't tell me why. What can be so bad?"

I bit my lip and shook my head. If Cheney didn't tell him, then I wouldn't either.

Sebastian sighed.

"I do have a question though. Why didn't our bond affect me my whole life?"

"The bond was with your elf half, which was dormant. Whatever spell you were under was strong enough to suppress the bond along with your memories."

"So if Cheney died while I was a human, would I have died too?"

He frowned. "I honestly don't know."

I chewed on my fingernail. *Interesting.* "But if I had died, he would have as well."

"Are you so angry that you're thinking about becoming human and killing him?"

I gave a one-shouldered shrug. If he killed Michael to scare me into staying with him, I might consider it.

Sebastian laughed. "Let me know if I need to look for a new job."

"It's not funny."

"Selene, you and Cheney fight. It's what you do, but neither of you are bad people. You'll work through whatever happened."

Though I had my doubts, he was missing the point. "It's not about our fight," I muttered.

He looked back at me, his expression serious again. "Care to elaborate?"

I shook my head.

He gave me a strange look and his expression softened. "You can trust me."

"Of course I can, you're only Cheney's advisor."

And like that, his face was back to normal. "Well, if you aren't staying here, then you better be able to transport yourself." He knelt across from me. "Elf magic is different from human magic in that it's innate. A part of you. You don't need words or circles to cast a spell."

I nodded, but it didn't make sense. I'd spent years learning how to cast and what he was suggesting broke all of the rules.

"It's like your telekinetic ability. How do you control it?"

"I, umm, hmm. Well, I guess I just, you know, will it to happen." It was harder to articulate than I imagined, but Sebastian nodded encouragingly. "So you want me to will myself into another room?"

"Yes, we'll start there." He stood up and offered me a hand.

I tried and nothing happened. I was so tired, and I didn't want to do this. I didn't want to do anything. My body ached like I'd run a marathon. I absently rubbed my breastbone and my mind drifted to Cheney drinking in the study. Where was he now? Was he thinking about me? My eyes drifted closed as I ignored Sebastian's incessant talking, and I could almost smell the dusty old books and Cheney's scent that was always laced with sandalwood. When I opened my eyes, I was standing behind the soft leather chair I'd sat in across from Cheney only yesterday. The room was dark and empty, silent as death. I didn't celebrate my success or hurry back to Sebastian. I walked along the bookcases, trailing my finger along the spines, trying to listen to my heart, but my heart wasn't talking. My mind, however, wouldn't be quiet. I sat in Cheney's chair and remembered his voice asking me if I'd ever loved him.

A pretty box made of interwoven pieces of various metals sat on the table beside me, gleaming even in the low light. I touched it lightly, trying to open it, but it was locked. I stared at it a moment, and then with a flick of my telekinetic mind, the lid popped up. The contents took a moment to register. I looked again. What the fuck?

The click of the door being shut made me jump out of the chair. I tore my gaze from the box. Cheney strolled toward me, his hands in his pocket. I backed up. *Oh shit.*

"Selene." His voice was soft. My eyes kept darting to the box then to him as I backed away, putting the chair between us. He frowned and followed my gaze. His eyes widened. "I can explain."

"Whose heart is that?"

His jaw clenched. "I'm not sure, but I think it is ..." He paused as if he had trouble saying the name. "Michael's."

My stomach lurched. I wanted to throw up, run away from him. "Why?" I kept moving back and he kept advancing. "How could you?"

His eyes widened even further, and he stopped. "You don't think I did this? What could I possibly have to gain by killing a human who was no longer in your life?"

"You tell me."

"Nothing. I have nothing to gain. This is why I wasn't in the gym with Sebastian this morning. I went to Sy's hoping to intercept you. I think you need to come back to the castle. It isn't safe for you out there."

"I'm not so sure it's safe for me in here," I said under my breath. Hurt filled his eyes.

"You don't mean that." He was in front of me in a blink, and I didn't have time to move away. The back of his hand brushed against my cheek and relief washed over me, but I fought against it. "I know somewhere in there you know you don't mean it."

I pressed my lips together, too confused to know anything.

He eased his arms around me and urged me closer. "I'm sorry for your loss, and I'm sorry I asked you to leave. Come back."

His touch opened up my lungs and let me breathe for the

first time since I'd walked away, but I struggled against him. "No," I said weakly, but he continued to hug me until I gave in and buried my face into his shoulder.

"I can protect you, Selene. I can take care of you."

I pushed away from him. "Like you did Michael?"

His arms fell to his sides. "That isn't fair."

"And being dead is?" I glanced back at the box. "What exactly happened? How did you get that?"

Cheney crossed his arms over his chest. "I don't appreciate your tone. What exactly have I done to lose your trust?"

I mimicked his stance. "Was I in love with you before we were bonded?"

He leaned back slightly and chewed on the side of his lip. "I like to think so." The wild intensity that laced his every look melted away and weariness replaced it. "The box was delivered here this morning. No one saw anything."

"Was there a note?"

"Not that I saw. Are you so certain it isn't your rebel friends doing this, trying to come between us because everything didn't go as planned?"

I wasn't certain of anything anymore. "Will my friends be safe here?"

He watched me for a moment. "Of course." He ran his hand through his hair, making it stick up in odd directions. "I was thinking about us last night. Did you mean it?"

"Mean what?"

"That you love me now. You haven't said it before. Not ever."

My feet felt heavy as if I couldn't run away even if I wanted to. "It's hard to say what's real and what's the bond."

"You know, the funny thing is everyone says elves aren't emotional. We're reserved and unfeeling. But you're the one who's unfeeling. You always have been. I have told you I love you a thousand times. Sure you can shed tears and turn a good phrase, but you can't even say it once."

He was right. I couldn't tell him I loved him. There were too many variables. "I won't say it until I'm sure I mean it. If that makes me unfeeling, then I guess that's what I am."

"Did you tell Michael you loved him?"

I shook my head.

"And the other man?"

I swallowed and looked away. I was pretty sure I *had* told Jaron I loved him.

He nodded. "Sebastian says I shouldn't let you leave, that we need you here."

"That's why I came back today. If you don't agree, I'll go." I pressed a hand to my chest where it hurt the most. "Maybe a little time apart will do us both some good."

He took a deep breath. "If it takes letting you leave again for you to see we do belong together, then I will. But Sebastian is right about keeping up appearances, at least until we know where we stand." He reached toward me then dropped his hand without making contact. "I know how I feel and it has nothing to do with the bond. I can forgive you, Selene, but this time you have to earn it."

"How?"

"I don't know." Cheney closed the distance between us. "Is there anything else you are keeping from me?"

Pros and cons about telling him anything further rolled through my mind. But in the end, I still couldn't believe Cheney was behind any of this. "Yeah. I've had more memories."

"Are they still hurting you? What have you remembered?"

"No, these memories aren't the same. They're being given back to me."

Cheney's eyebrows pulled together. "What do you mean 'given back'?"

"Apparently, before the changeling spell was cast, I stored all my memories with someone else."

He sat in his chair. "That doesn't make any sense. It isn't possible."

I shrugged. "What about any of this makes sense?" The gleam of the box caught my eye and a lump rose in my throat. "I should go back to Sy's."

"Will you be back tomorrow?"

I looked over my shoulder. "Yeah. No matter what it looks like or what you think, I don't want to hurt you. I just want to understand what's happening. I still believe in you and think you will make a wonderful Erlking. You will always have my full support."

"These memories, are you sure you can trust them?"

I shook my head. "I'm not sure of anything."

Cheney was in front of me in a blink. He ran his hand over my hair, his eyes nearly pleading. "Stay."

I could only shake my head.

"I need the finger," I told Sy as I appeared in his bar, clutching a stool to steady myself against the dizziness.

His eyes flickered to each person in the room. "You transported. Good job, but don't transport into here. Keep it in the back or outside."

"Fine. The finger," I said impatiently.

"We discussed this, Selene."

I planted both hands on the bar and leaned toward him. "Michael is dead." I didn't mention that was probably because they wouldn't let me go to him. Now wasn't the time to point fingers.

Sy stopped wiping down the counter. "Are you sure?"

"No. That's why I need the finger." I gave him a quick rundown of what had transpired. "Do you think I was wrong to leave my coven with him?"

Sy ran his hand over his buzz cut. "If Cheney isn't involved, like he claims, the castle is the safest spot for them. And even if he does have something to do with this, he obviously wants you to keep coming back to him. With your coven there, you will. I bet they're safe."

"They better be. Now, where's the finger?"

"Holden has it. I figured you'd snoop until you found it, so I sent it back with him."

"Great." I glared at him.

"We'll get it. Just relax."

It annoyed me that no one in this world seemed overly concerned about a dead human. What was wrong with these people?

"While you wait, you can learn. Step behind the bar." He gave me a lopsided grin that was impossible to scowl at.

Bartending wasn't so hard. Sy didn't mix drinks so I didn't have to memorize anything. He told me anyone who came in looking for Sex on the Beach was in the wrong bar.

We had straight alcohol or beer, no mixers. He introduced me to a little group of strange looking creatures who worked in the kitchen. He said they could and would make anything anyone asked for. Other than that, all I had to do was answer the phone and post the bounties on the wall across from the bar as they came through.

"Oh, and remove anyone who starts a fight. Can you handle that?"

"I think so."

"Great. You can work with me tonight, and we'll see how you do."

The thing about the Office was that it was never empty. Someone was always sitting at a table waiting for that perfect hunt, no matter what time of day it was. Unless Sy closed the bar down like he had the couple times we had meetings, there was always somebody lurking in the shadows. "Who filled in for you when you came to see me the first time?"

Sy smiled at me mischievously. "No one."

"Did you close down?"

He shook his head. "We rarely ever close."

"And you're open 24/7, but you work alone?"

"Bounties aren't going to find themselves, nor do they keep to business hours. This is often life or death, Selene."

"Then I don't understand. How?"

"Are you thinking about a career change?" He winked and laughed. "Let's see how you do tonight before I start spilling the secrets of my profession."

We stood behind the bar chatting until the door opened. A petite woman with white blonde hair down to her butt came through. "Frost. How'd it go?" Sy said to her.

She turned, lifted a thin ebony eyebrow and regarded us

with ice blue eyes as she adjusted her black gloves. "Taken care of. Who's the new girl?"

"This is Selene. Selene, this is Frost."

I smiled and Frost turned and walked away. "Glad to see everyone is so friendly." I scrunched my nose. "She doesn't look like much of a bounty hunter. At least Femi looks like she can kick someone's ass. She looks like a Barbie."

Sy crossed his arms. "Frost is a necromancer. She's the real deal."

I looked at her with new appreciation. Necromancers controlled the dead. How she applied that to bounty hunting I had no idea, but most people would consider what she did black magic. She was definitely fringe. I watched her until the door opened again. This time a tall bald man with hunched shoulders walked through. Tattoos crawled up his neck and sleeved his arms down to his wrists. I turned to where Sy had been, but he was gone. I looked back and the scary man stood in front of me.

"Who are you?"

"Selene. What can I get you?"

"Whiskey."

I grabbed a glass and the bottle.

"And a piece of your sweet ass."

I took in his smug smile as I slid the drink in front of him. Then I flicked my fingers at my side, imagining his stupid thick silver chain tightening around his neck. His smile faltered and his fingers inched up to pull it away, but the chain tightened until his face began to turn blue. I leaned in close and whispered in his ear. "Next time you talk down to me, I won't stop." I snapped my fingers and the necklace went slack.

He glared at me, coughing as he slapped money on the counter.

"What, no tip?" I called after him and laughed to myself. This wasn't so bad. I felt powerful behind the bar. Some of the constant anger inside of me basked in the glow of exerting my power over others.

"You'll do just fine," Sy said behind me.

"Thanks for disappearing."

"I had to see how you would do when I'm not here. You passed."

We worked side by side, talking about nothing. Sy showed me how to blend in and listen. We watched the board, noting who took which bounties and which ones were left behind. He said this told which way the wind was blowing and what races to distance yourself from. It was like a big social experiment, and Sy was an expert at reading everyone who came in. He knew them all by name and his silver eyes darted everywhere, taking in everything. Jaron came in a few hours later, changing the atmosphere in the bar.

"Thanks for your help tonight." Sy winked at me, knowing I was about to abandon him.

Jaron followed me to the living room without a word until he closed the door. He looked me up and down. "You look bad."

My eyebrows furrowed. Then what he meant dawned on me. My hand went to my chest. The separation was wearing me down. "I'm okay."

He moved closer. "There are circles under your eyes—eyes that are completely bloodshot. You looked stressed. So unlike you, Selene"

Today came back to me. I was as bad as Sy and Cheney. I forgot about Michael. A little distraction and he was as good as gone from my mind. My shoulders dropped and I sat down. "Michael is dead."

Jaron sat beside me. "How do you know?"

"I found his heart. At least I think it was his heart." His hand grazed my knee. "I just don't know why anyone would do this. Michael wasn't even a part of this world."

Jaron leaned back. "This wasn't about him. It was about you."

"That makes me feel better," I grumbled.

Jaron leaned his muscular forearms on his knees. "I'm not here to make you feel better. I'm here to bring you back."

"Why?"

Those gray eyes met mine, seeing through me. "I'm not saying I want you back. I'm tired of carrying pieces of you with me. You need to take back your memories and decide once and for all what the hell you want. I don't care if it's Cheney or a human—"

"Or you?" I said softly, still trying to figure out how he felt.

He frowned. "I'm not here for your entertainment. We had a good run, Selene, but it needs to end."

I sucked in a breath. Part of me withered at Jaron's words. I struggled to refocus. "How do the memories work? Do you see them with me?"

"You laced your life onto the memories we shared. I cannot see everything that comes with them, but it does bring those moments to mind."

"Then why don't you just give me the last memory, then I'll remember everything before it."

He shook his head. "I don't control which memories you get or how often we have to do this to get them all back. You set all of this up, not me. And you never explained anything to me."

Jaron and I were so close in my memories. He taught me to survive, showed me what the world was like. Life with Sy and Aunt Lorelei had verged on idyllic, and the real world only offered disappointment. Jaron had always been there to pick me up and dust me off. He was an important person to me, and I knew that in a place that was untouched by the bond I shared with Cheney. I studied his carefully guarded face. "Is it hard to be here with me?"

His lips curled. "I moved on. What, did you believe I would wait?" His voice was soft and made my stomach flutter.

I did think he would wait. In every memory, every recalled feeling, Jaron always being there was the one constant. I'd never had a single doubt that he'd still be here when I came back—*and here he is,* a voice insisted in my head, refusing to believe we couldn't have him back if we chose him. I pressed my lips together. "I guess I didn't think about it." I intended to drop the subject, but my mouth kept moving despite my best intentions. "Who is she?"

He raised an eyebrow. "Are you ready for your memory? I don't have all night."

I bit back the string of questions I wanted to throw at him and nodded. Jaron wrapped his fingers round the back of my neck. I didn't have a right to expect anything else from him, no matter what the other half of me believed.

His lips crushed into mine. I responded, though my own thoughts kept drifting back to him moving on. He couldn't move on. I needed him. I tried to tamp down the thoughts and kissed him back even harder, my arms around his neck.

He pulled back slightly. "It isn't working."

"Maybe I have too much on my mind."

His gaze seared into me. "Deeper. It has to be deeper." As he came toward me, I lay back on the couch, torn about how far I was willing to let this go. Part of me filled with triumph because he never could resist me, and the other part didn't want to keep toying with people's feelings. His gray eyes darkened with desire as he looked over me. I traced my fingers down the side of his face and he kissed me again softly, the weight of his body pressing down on me. He trailed a line of kisses down one side of my neck and back up the other. I arched my back, pressing against him. His tongue ran the seam of my mouth, asking for entrance. I complied, my mind going blissfully still, allowing Jaron to fill my senses.

ELEVEN

I slammed the door to Jaron's house open. "You win," I yelled. It was the middle of the night, but I didn't care. I stood with my arms crossed over my chest and listened to the rustling movements as he came to me. When Jaron came into sight, I almost resented him as much as I loved him. He was making me do this.

He looked at me, his face impassive. "I told you not to come back."

"I left him." My skin hummed with energy, but I didn't care. I was furious and glad to be home. Cheney wasn't bad to me, but he did do an annoyingly good job thwarting my efforts to make him choose between me and his father. The only way to move us forward was to become a changeling, but Jaron had made it clear that if I went that route, he was done, so I left Cheney, deserted my plan. I needed Jaron.

He mirrored my stance, crossing his arms over his big chest peppered with dark hair, so unlike an elf. "Why?"

"I can live without a lot of things, Jaron. I don't need my family, I don't need love, I don't need to be happy, but I need you. And I hate you for it."

He tilted his head back. "Why?" he asked again, making me want to groan.

"Without you, I don't know who I am."

"You're young, Selene. I wager you don't know who you are, even with me."

I shrugged. Like that mattered. I was giving him what he wanted. I was here, elves be damned. We would do this the old-fashioned way and defeat them in a battle rather than with a scheme. People would die, but I would have Jaron.

"You've spent your life defining yourself by others. By who did and did not love you. You've twisted yourself into so many knots, I'm not sure you can ever untie them all."

"And you're perfect, Jaron?" I raised an eyebrow. *"You cannot allow yourself to live or even feel deeply. And why is that? Why do you have to be alone? Why did you make me love you if you insist on pushing me away? I may define myself by others, but at least I have other people I care about more than myself."*

He growled, but I wasn't scared. Jaron wouldn't hurt me. I knew that as well as I knew my own reflection. He had proven it so many times. *"I feel plenty, but I have self-control. You are young and the prince loves you. Go back to him, have children, be happy, and leave me in peace. You will get the same ending you desire."*

"No."

"I cannot give you what you want."

"Who cares? You're getting what you want—me." I went to him, no longer caring if he came to me like I'd sworn to myself I would make him do.

He smiled. *"I've never known anyone quite so full of herself."* He took a small step toward me. *"It's the confidence of someone used to getting what she wants, no matter what the cost. You say you can let this go, but can you? Can you move past your own desires?"*

"Can you?" I asked, running a hand down his chest to the elastic waist of his pajama bottoms.

Jarons's eyes darkened and he closed the rest of the distance.

I opened my eyes and Jaron was gone. I lay on the couch alone, clothes rumpled but still on. I pressed a hand to my lips and recalled the feeling of his mouth against mine. My chest ached for the millionth time for Cheney, and for the millionth time I cursed the stupid bond. Seriously, how did I get from point A to point B on this? I was back with Jaron. I had given up. I recalled Cheney telling me I'd left him for a year, but I returned . . . Why did I go back? What happened to change things? I sat up, groaning in frustration that Jaron, the one person who could tell me, had left.

Elf Selene may not have been the psycho I originally thought she was. I understood her motives regarding Cheney better now, and apparently she struggled to keep up appearances with him. But she was an idiot. Even remembering the vast majority of my elf life, I still couldn't fathom how we ended up where we did. She loved Jaron, so why did she leave him? Better yet, why would she bond with Cheney and give her memories to Jaron? What was I missing?

"You okay?" Sy asked from the doorway.

"Yeah." I stood up, straightening my short, cream-colored dress. "Where's Jaron?" I smoothed my hair as I looked up at Sy.

"He took off." Sy grinned. "What were you two doin'?"

I pressed my kiss-swollen lips together to keep from

smiling. "Retrieving memories."

"I bet."

"He's moved on—"

"Yeah," Sy said with incredulity. "Right on out the door. That was not the scowl of someone who has let go of the past. What about you? Have you moved on?"

"I'm catching up with the past. It left me behind."

"Hmph." He shook his head and walked back out.

I followed closely behind. "What does that mean?"

Sy refilled a couple drinks before he answered. "You don't want to choose between them, so you're using not remembering as an excuse. You enjoy having them fight over you."

"That isn't true! I don't know them. How could I choose?" I jammed my hands against my hips. "Jaron barely talks to me and anything I feel for Cheney is so muddled I can't begin to make it out."

"But you know what you feel for Jaron?" Sy smiled. "Is my baby cousin in looovvee?"

"Oh my God, shut up." I turned away from him, laughing, and practically bumped into Holden. "Holy smokes, when did you get here?" I clamped my hand to my chest.

Holden actually smiled. Who knew he had teeth? "So you're in love?" he said, his eyes softening ever so slightly along the edges.

"Hardly." I stammered. I had no idea what I felt and I certainly wasn't discussing it with him. "Do you have the finger?"

"Perhaps. Why do you need it?"

"Michael's dead. We're going to find out where the rest

of his body is."

Holden shrugged and pulled the bag from his inside pocket. Sy waved us toward the back room. "I'm running a business here."

"Where's Olivia?" I asked, scanning the small apartment for the right spot.

"Out," Holden said, his voice laced with suspicion.

I glanced back at him. "Just making conversation." *Geez.* "She doesn't mind you being here with me?"

Holden gave me the most perplexed look I had ever seen. "Why would she mind? She's the one who wanted me to help you."

My cheeks warmed with my own ego staring me in the face. I wasn't used to being dismissed quite so easily. I made myself busy and moved the coffee table out of the way. Then I dug a piece of chalk out of my purse and drew a circle on the stone floor. Holden stood back watching me. "Would you ask Sy if he has a candle and salt?"

When I was satisfied with the circle, I retrieved a crystal I kept on my keychain and got a bowl of water. Holden came back with both items in hand. "I'm not going to chant."

I laughed. "You don't have to. Just be quiet."

"That I can do." He leaned against the wall as I placed the finger in the center and created my circle of protection, calling on the elements. When I was finished, I stood, letting the energy wash over me.

"Earth bone, dying flesh, show me where this spirit rests. Let the blood be my guide to where this body resides." I placed the finger in a bowl and repeated the spell three more times before dipping the crystal in the water and willing all of my energy into it. The crystal turned red and hummed.

Pressure built in the air until my ears popped. I grounded the rest of my energy and exited the circle.

"Holden stood up straight. "So, where are we going?"

"I don't know. We have to follow the crystal."

Holden's laugh was derisive. "What do you think that will do? He could be anywhere. What are the odds that body is in Chicago?"

I twirled my hair, thinking my way around this. "Perhaps I can transport there. I'm connected to the crystal. I can feel it, so maybe it will take me to him."

Holden stood motionless, staring "I can't let you do that. Liv wouldn't be happy."

I held out my hand. "Then come with me."

His lip rose in something resembling disgust and his hand hesitated over the top of mine. All expression drained from his face as he lowered his hand the rest of the way. I squeezed my eyes shut and clutched the crystal in my other hand, willing with all of my heart and soul to go where the crystal led.

"This is where he is?" Holden asked and I opened my eyes. We stood outside of the ruins of the church Cheney took me to when he told me about his sister.

"I hope not," I whispered. I couldn't believe Cheney would tell me a story like that then kill Michael here.

"Only one way to find out." Holden pulled a gun from the back of his pants and walked inside. I followed him, wringing my hands. My eyes adjusted quickly to the dark. "I can't see a damn thing," Holden said.

I scanned the room. "No one's here." I walked slowly toward the front until his fingers curled around my arm.

"We're leaving."

"What? No. What if his body is here now? That doesn't mean it will be in the morning."

Holden let out a huffy breath. "I don't care. I can't see. We're leaving."

"Just a quick look around." I walked forward. He trailed behind me but managed to always keep me within reach. The front of the ruin held a crumbling stone altar oozing some sort of dark substance from over its top. I had my suspicion about what it was but couldn't see well enough to determine a color. "Looks like blood," I whispered.

We walked around the stone mound and found Michael. His face was slack and waxy, eyes open, staring lifelessly at the sky. There was a gaping hole in his chest where his heart used to be. I choked back a sob and a stronger, colder part of me refused to turn away. Instead I squatted down in front of the body and looked it over the best I could, describing what I found to Holden. He had me scan the room one more time to make sure we were alone. When I gave him the all clear, he pulled out his cell phone and used the light to illuminate the body.

After a moment he nodded. "Okay, we found him, let's go."

I crossed my arms. "We aren't leaving him here."

"That's exactly what we're doing."

"Why?"

"First, we need to come back in the daylight. Second, as far as we know, whoever took him doesn't know we've found the body yet. That gives us the opportunity to watch the church and see who else comes here."

Despite not wanting to admit it, his logic made sense. "Do you think it's Cheney?"

Holden shrugged. "I don't have an opinion." He took my arm and pulled me away from the body.

"Everyone has an opinion."

"Not me." He stopped in the center of the aisle. "Go back to the Office." He waited for me to leave with a stony expression.

"Geez, you're bossy," I grumbled as I went back to Sy's. I expected Holden to transport with me, but he let go of my arm just before I left. I stood in Sy's living room, frowning. Where the hell was he? A moment later a thick black smoke filled the room, but before I could panic it formed into Holden. "I didn't know jinn could transport."

"They can't," he said flatly. "Does it actually matter who did this?"

My eyebrows pulled together. "Of course."

He nodded. "You strung along two men who are used to getting their way before you became a changeling. Now the human you were engaged to is dead. They're the two most likely suspects. Unless there were others…"

"Not that I know of." I frowned. "But Michael and I were over. How could he matter?"

Holden gave me a look that said it definitely mattered.

"Well, if this is all about jealousy, why aren't they trying to kill each other?"

"They are. Cheney wants to kill the rebel leader, but when you said that was you, he didn't lock you away and he didn't drop the idea of killing your partner. He still intends to kill Jaron as soon as he finds out who he is. And Jaron wanted you to kill Cheney and take control. Neither of them is willing to turn the other cheek."

"So I can't trust either of them?"

He shrugged. "Do what you want."

I flopped down on the couch and crossed my legs. "You aren't very good at giving advice."

"I don't care how you live your life so long as you don't involve Liv in whatever you have going on. If you want to kill Cheney and take the crown, fine. If you want to publicly execute Jaron and take the crown, more power to you. If you want to leave them both and get the fuck out of here, I'll make Baker help you. Just make up your damn mind."

I stared at him for a long moment. I couldn't decide if he was an awesome friend to have or just mean. "I don't think it's either of them."

"Because you have reason or because you don't want it to be?" He lifted an eyebrow. "Look, I never wanted to get involved in any of this. I don't care about what's happening to you." He gave me a pointed look. "However, I'm here and I'm going to help you because Olivia cares. Loving someone else changes you. You do things and want things you never thought you would."

"What's your point?"

He glowered. "My point is, love makes you do stupid things that are against all sense, reason, and character. No matter what you think you know, you can never really anticipate what someone you love is capable of."

"So who can I trust?"

Holden rolled his eyes. "The less people you trust the better."

"Well, you're just a ray of sunshine."

Holden smirked. "Maybe, but I'm still alive."

"And if Olivia were here, what advice would she give me?"

He shook his head. "To follow your heart, but trust me, that only leads to trouble. Olivia is the last person you should take advice from. She only sees the good in people."

Holden started for the door before turning around. "Do you still want to break the bond?"

I nodded.

"Baker knows someone he thinks can do it. I'll send him here tomorrow."

"Thank you."

Holden walked out and nervous excitement nearly made me forget the dull ache. One day from now and I would be free.

TWELVE

"Where's your focus?" Sebastian asked as he reached down to help me off the ground.

I ignored his hand and his comment as I pushed myself up, despite my protesting muscles. "Again."

Sebastian stepped back. "No. Enough for today."

Despite Sy's objections, I'd returned to the castle like everything was normal. Cheney and I were pole fighting on a balance beam, but I couldn't hold my attention long enough to compete. My mind kept drifting back to Michael's lifeless form and wondering if Holden would find anything this morning. Breaking the bond tonight was never far from my mind either. And before I knew it I'd be on the floor with both men staring down at me. "Again."

Cheney frowned and jumped down from the beam. "Sebastian's right. You're half dead." He put his arm over my shoulder and I felt a moment of peace. I hated that he had that effect on me, but it wouldn't be for much longer.

"Fine. If you guys are quitting, I'm going to hang out with the girls." I charged toward the door. I needed to be away from him and the temptation of relief before I started second guessing my decision. Cheney fell into step with me.

"Come with me for a moment."

"Where are we going?"

"It's a surprise," he said, a mischievous glint in his eyes. I hesitated. I didn't want him to give me things. "Trust me."

That was the kicker, wasn't it? I didn't trust him. I couldn't. I wanted to believe in Cheney, but my memories struggled with what the bond made me feel, leaving me in a great ball of confusion. I followed him toward his office, my throat dry. When we walked through the door I immediately recognized the elf inside.

I stopped and stared.

"Selene," said the musical voice that should have been familiar, but it wasn't.

"Tahlik," I said coldly and he flinched.

"So you do remember him," Cheney said.

I glanced over. "I told you I didn't want to see him."

"The last time we met, Selene, things were different—"

I held up a hand to stop him. "You made your position clear." I turned and walked away from them both. How could Cheney blindside me like that? This time he didn't come after me. I stormed down the hallways until I got to the girls' quarters. I brushed past the guard standing outside of their room and flopped down on the couch next to Devin, who looked as exhausted as I felt. "Have you heard anything about Michael?" Leslie asked.

I looked up into four sets of concerned eyes. "He's dead." I chewed on my thumbnail and stared toward the door. How could Cheney bring my father here on top of everything? I'd wanted a relationship with him since I was a child, but when he brushed me away as if I were nothing my idealized vision of him was stripped from me. Who could I trust? Cheney said the elves had forgotten about that church and that he was the only one who went there. Would he have left a body there for me to find? It seemed so obvious.

"What the hell is wrong with you, Selene?"

Startled, I whipped around to Jessica. "Nothing. Why?"

"Exactly." She threw up her hands. "You've always been reserved, but this is ridiculous. You were with Michael for months and now you have no feelings about him being dead? Why are we staying here, but you're not?"

I looked around the rest of the group, completely flabbergasted.

"I think what Jessica means is that you aren't talking to us. You used to let us in. You would have told us about Michael. Now even when you sit near us, you're off in your own world," Devin explained, patting my leg. "I am still having dreams. I don't understand them, but whoever did this isn't done yet."

Katrina didn't say anything but gave me a look saying I needed to fill them in.

"You've changed," Leslie said.

"And not for the better," Jessica grumbled.

"Enough, Jess." Leslie threw a pillow at her. "We love you, Selene. We just want you to trust us like you used to."

I sighed. They were right. I had been a bad friend. "I'm sorry. I do trust all of you. There's just so much going on right now, and I'm not sure we can talk here." I widened my eyes for emphasis.

"I thought the castle was safe. That's why you wanted to bring us here, right?" Concern colored Devin's face.

I needed to explain so much to them, but I couldn't say half of it here. "Do you guys want to go for a walk?" Confusion washed across their faces, but I nodded toward the door and smiled. Slowly they all got up and followed me out. I waved the guard away when he went to follow us.

He shook his head. "The Erlking decreed I am not to leave them."

"And I'm telling you to go." I glared at him, but the guard didn't budge.

"What's going on?" Cheney's voice came from behind me.

I turned my glare to him. "Your guards don't take orders from a lowly half-elf."

Cheney's shocked gaze met my angry one, but he didn't say anything. He waved the guard away.

"We're going for a walk." I turned to leave and he caught my arm.

"Your father is still waiting for you." My friends exchanged confused glances at Cheney's words.

"Then he will wait longer."

Outside it was easier to breathe. I led them deep into the surrounding forest until I felt we could safely be ourselves.

"I'm sorry I've been absent."

"I thought your father was dead," Devin said.

I frowned. "No, he's not dead. He just didn't want anything to do with me after my mother died." I launched into the whole story, sharing everything about Cheney and Jaron, though I left his name out of things. They listened in silence as I spoke, a rare feat for them. When I finally finished, Katrina was the first to respond.

She smiled. "Your life went from like zero to hot mess in about 2.3 seconds."

"So this isn't your dad, it's the elf's dad," Jessica said.

I laughed and the icy shell that had been surrounding me

cracked. I knew why they thought I'd changed. As my memories came back, I'd let too much distance grow between me and the people who kept me grounded. I was inadvertently letting the elf half win. I already felt my burden lift just by talking to them.

"Well, this is great. Now you have family again." Devin hugged me.

"So what happened to Michael?" Jessica asked.

"I don't know. I have friends looking into it."

"Again with the mysterious 'friends,'" Kat griped, but her smile said she was joking.

"But you think Cheney could be involved?" Leslie asked.

"It would make sense, but I'm having trouble believing he'd do something like this."

"What can we do to help?" Devin asked.

A cheesy grin covered my face. "I love you guys, have I mentioned that? If I start pulling away again, call me out. Call me out every time." I wanted to hug them for reminding me who I was and what was important. "Other than that, keep doing what you've been doing. Keep your eyes and ears open, and let me know if anything suspicious happens."

"Can do," Leslie said.

"And be careful. If someone here is involved, they have no qualms about killing humans." I looked back toward the castle. Would breaking the bond change things? Right now, if I died, so did Cheney. If Cheney was behind this, was I destroying my only layer of protection? "And be ready to leave any minute."

We went back before nightfall. I slowly made my way to the room where my father was, on the off chance he hadn't left, while the girls headed off in pairs in different directions back to their quarters, hoping to be able to eavesdrop on more people. I had my doubts that noisy, clumsy humans would ever get the drop on elves, but at least it kept them busy.

I opened the door slowly. Tahlik was still there, sipping a drink across from Cheney. Cheney smiled when I walked in. "I told you she'd come," he said and Tahlik looked up.

"I'm sorry I left so abruptly before."

"I wanted many times to see you, Selene. You must understand that."

I struggled to keep a bitter smile from my lips. "Must I?" I walked over to them and Cheney gave me his chair before retrieving another. "Because I don't."

Tahlik stared at me. "You are so much like your mother—always right to the point. But remember, dear, I am your father. You should show me respect."

I shook my head. "You aren't my father. Edward Warren was my father. He died when I was seven, but at least he was there. At least he was a part of my life. You. Well, you were a sperm donor."

"I think we're done here," Tahlik said.

"Selene." Cheney frowned.

"What? He isn't my father. Aunt Lorelei raised me as an elf and Edward and Jane Warren raised me as a human until my grandmother took over. Where does Tahlik fit in? He never once came to find me. Not one birthday card or phone call."

"I could not. The king didn't allow it of any of the nobles. I had a family to think of."

My anger boiled, threatening to erupt. Why would he care for me when he had a more important family to consider? "Well that didn't stop you from having an affair with a human."

He glared at me. "We all have human conquests, even the king. We do not claim the children. It isn't the way it is done." He looked to Cheney for support.

"So how about you stop with the hypocrisy and the father crap and quit expecting me to claim *you*." I glared.

Cheney swallowed uncomfortably. "Maybe this was a bad idea."

"Oh no," I interrupted. "It's a fabulous idea, Cheney, love. Just think. You probably have half-siblings out there that you don't know. Should we find them?"

"Selene—"

"No, no. Please, Tahlik, tell us. Who was the king fucking?"

"I only remember one from the—"

"Enough," Cheney snapped. "We aren't here to talk about my family."

"No. We're just forcing mine on me." I gave him a tight smile.

Tahlik sighed. "Selene, I apologize if my absence hurt you. I am happy you and the new Erlking have found love in one another, but I do not know what you want from me. If you will not let go of the past, how can I be a part of your future?"

"You can't be."

Tahlik nodded and stood up. I immediately felt bad for being mean, but I couldn't let him in. I couldn't open myself up for more pain with everything already on the line. When the door shut, Cheney leaned forward. "That didn't go as I thought."

"I told you not to bring him here." I stared at my feet, letting my elf half raise a wall against my emotions.

Cheney kissed the top of my head. "I'm sorry. I should have listened. I just wanted to do something nice for you."

I took his hand. I was so tired of fighting and not trusting anyone. That way of living might work for Holden, but it didn't for me. Cheney started to speak again, but the door opened. He looked up impatiently. "What?"

"Um." An uncomfortable looking guard cleared his throat. "I apologize for the interruption, your majesty, but Sebastian sent me. He said it is urgent."

Cheney looked down at me. "I should probably go."

I nodded and stood. "I'll come with you." We followed the guard down to the gardens. Sebastian stood at the entrance, waiting.

He shifted as we approached. "Selene, you should go back inside."

"Yeah, right." I made a face. "What's going on?"

He shook his head and looked at Cheney. "Send her inside."

Cheney's eyebrows shot up. "Selene and I have no secrets." A short bitter laugh sputtered from Sebastian's lips. Cheney gave him a withering look, laced with warning. "What do you need?" His voice was cold, verging on hostile.

Sebastian composed himself immediately and nodded

toward the garden surrounded by tall hedges. Cheney rolled his eyes and led the way through the opening. I fell in line behind him and Sebastian followed me. I glanced back at him, trying to decipher what exactly happened. Sebastian knew something. I had to get him to talk to me. His eyes met mine, and he shook his head ever so slightly as if he knew exactly what I was thinking. Sebastian suddenly became a lot more interesting.

I smashed into Cheney, who had stopped dead. He absorbed the blow and didn't budge forward. "Take her back inside."

THIRTEEN

Sebastian made no move toward me. "You have no secrets," he said levelly, and Cheney turned to glare at him.

I caught sight of a foot just beyond Cheney. I knew that shoe. I stepped around the two of them to see Michael laid out on the stone garden bench. How had he gotten here? And if Cheney was responsible for the murder, why would he bring the body to his own castle? Why would he originally leave the body in a place we'd visited together? It didn't make sense. Despite the possible motive, Cheney was probably innocent. Unless he was doing this because I found the heart and upset whatever plan he'd had. Was he trying to divert suspicion by pointing the finger at himself?

Cheney took hold of my shoulders and turned me toward him. His gold eyes softened with empathy. "I am very sorry, Selene."

His words made me realize I wasn't reacting as I should. I felt strangely disconnected. I was sad Michael's life had been snuffed out so early, yes—but I was over the initial horror because Holden and I had already discovered his body, though Cheney didn't know that. The mystery of who took Michael's life and why were the only things on my mind.

"Are you okay? Talk to me." Cheney rubbed his hands up and down my arms as I continued to stare at him, trying to fathom if this man before me would kill an innocent person to assure I'd stay with him. I looked over to Sebastian. His face was tight and his eyes were worried. "Go inside with Sebastian. I'll take care of everything," Cheney tried again.

I squirmed out of his grasp, not knowing what to think or feel. "I'm fine." I glanced back at the body. "I take it no one knows anything about how he ended up here."

Surprise replaced worry and sympathy on their faces. Sebastian's head tilted to the side as he studied me, and Cheney narrowed his eyes. "Selene, love, you don't seem overly..." he looked over at the body and then back to me, "bothered."

"How upset would you like me to be, Cheney?" I glared at him, anger burning away any traces of sadness. "Please, tell me how you think I should react. It isn't like I didn't know he was dead. You had his *heart*."

I headed toward the body, needing to see it in daylight. I wondered if there was a spell that could help me find his killer. I squatted down and really inspected him. He looked like a wax imitation. My hand drifted toward his clenched fist, but I couldn't bring myself to touch him. The flesh beneath his left eye was bruised, but besides that, the only other mark I could see was the gaping hole in this chest. Something was off.

Sebastian joined me. "There's no odor." He spoke without inflection.

"That's strange, isn't it?"

"I would think there should be a smell, yes."

I nodded and stared some more. . Michael had been dead

at least two days, yet he wasn't decomposing. "Have you touched him?"

"No."

It had to be magic. Touching the body would probably dissolve the spell.

"I don't know what the two of you think you're going to learn staring at a dead human. It's macabre," Cheney said crossly, pacing in front of us.

"I wouldn't want to waste your time, Erlking. Why don't you go inside? We'll take care of this."

He whirled toward me. I could feel his eyes drilling into me as I continued looking for clues and anomalies. "That's what all of this is about, isn't it?" he said softly. "You're still mad I wouldn't help look for him. You are blaming me, aren't you?" He sounded affronted and hurt.

I eased myself up and rolled my shoulders back. "I haven't blamed anyone for anything. I'm just looking for answers."

He threw his arms up. "There are no answers here. Despite everything that has happened, I would never hurt you or allow you to be hurt." He ran his hands through his hair. "You know that, right?"

I wanted so very much to believe what he was saying, but a voice in my mind reminded me that Cheney had only told me the bits and pieces he wanted me to know since I'd met him. My hesitation seemed to be answer enough for him. He turned and stalked back toward the castle. My gaze followed him until he was completely gone.

"You've remembered." Sebastian's voice was soft and low behind me. "That's why you left."

I furrowed my eyebrows in response, not trusting my

voice, and tried to look as innocent as possible.

He stared at me, not fooled. "But have you remembered everything?"

"I don't know what you're talking about." I crossed my arms over my chest.

"You don't remember me at all, do you?"

I thought hard about Sebastian because Cheney had said we were friends. I remembered my time with Cheney, but I had no previous memories of Sebastian. Why would he be missing? And if he was missing, who and what else also were? "That's absurd."

"Is it? I see more and more of the old you peeking through. You even move like an elf now."

I frowned, not liking the truth in his words. I didn't want to lose me. "I thought you liked me better as a human."

He nodded. "Your human personality is better for Cheney, but you are who you are."

"And just who's that, Sebastian?"

A ghost of a smile graced his lips. "The changeling."

I didn't quite understand what he was getting at. Did he want me to remember or to stay as I was? Either way, maybe he could shed some light on my remaining memory gaps. "Why did I become a changeling?"

He pulled his eyebrows together in thought. "Only you really know the answer to that. I only know what you and Cheney told me."

"And what was that?"

He glanced around to make sure no one else was in earshot and I leaned toward him, eager to hear whatever he had to say. "To protect you. To bring you back."

"Back from what? From the rebels?"

He sighed. "This is not the place to discuss this. The Erlking has made it clear I am not to discuss your past with you."

A sliver of ice-cold anger impaled me. "Then obviously he has something to hide."

"You are focusing on the wrong things. You always have. He loves you, Selene. He would do anything for you if you would love him back." His jaw clenched for a moment. "There can be peace," he hissed.

Yes, it was the "anything" part that scared me most. "Well, he didn't help me find Michael." I took a deep breath and pushed past my questions. "There are more important issues at the moment, like who did this to Michael and why was he brought here. Oh, and what are we going to do with the body?"

Sebastian rubbed his hand over his forehead. "He could just disappear. That would be the easiest solution."

I pursed my lips. "Don't you have a heart?" A sputtering laugh broke through his serious exterior and I elbowed him. "Not funny."

"What would you suggest?"

"We should turn him over to the authorities."

"The *human* authorities?"

I nodded.

Sebastian didn't even pretend to consider it. "No. Too dangerous. There is one rule in the Abyss: humans can never know."

"I don't think anyone will jump to a supernatural explanation. We'll be okay."

He shrugged. "So long as it doesn't lead back to us, I have no objection." He hunched down by the body again.

"How do you want to do this?"

I wrinkled my nose. All I knew about cops and dead bodies came from police dramas on TV. "I'll call Femi. She has experience with stuff like this. And I'm going to check Grandma's Book of Shadows. Make sure no one touches Michael." I hurried back into the castle and texted Femi, not watching where I was going, yet somehow still managing to weave through the people in the castle and make it back to the private quarters, where my coven was staying, without looking up or running into anyone. Was this what Sebastian meant by moving like an elf? I slipped into the room, which, surprisingly, was unguarded.

The girls were nowhere to be seen—but Cheney was there. I skidded to a stop. "We need to talk." His voice was authoritative and almost grave.

I flippantly waved my hand in the air. "No time. I have to get back to Sebastian and the body. Femi is on her way too." My eyes darted around the room, seeking the book I'd last seen with Devin in here.

"Selene, sit down." He took me by the shoulders and sat me on the couch before I could even think about resisting.

"What is wrong with you? I know you don't care about Michael, but I do," I snapped, about to stand up again.

"I will tie you down if I have to." He lifted an eyebrow and I flopped back down, crossing my arms over my chest.

"I would transport out," I grumbled.

"Not inside the castle. It's warded against that."

"No, it isn't. I learned to transport in the castle."

Cheney gave me an impatient look. "The barriers were removed while you were training and put back up afterward. Haven't you noticed everyone goes outside to leave, including you?"

I frowned. He was right. I did it without thinking about it. I arrived outside the castle and left the same way. "Fine, whatever. Where are my friends?"

An emotion I couldn't quite place rippled over his face. "I sent them to their rooms with a guard. They're not to leave their chambers without a guard present for the rest of their stay."

Everything in me went still. Something was wrong. I stared at him, too afraid to ask what happened. Was someone caught snooping?

"Devin was taken," he said softly.

"Taken where?" I whispered, still not comprehending.

Cheney produced a letter that looked too familiar. My heart beat like it would explode. I leaned away from the slip of paper as he offered it to me. "No, no, no..." My hands formed helpless fists. The room began to shake.

Cheney knelt in front of me, taking my face gently between his hands. "Destroying the castle won't bring her back, and it will hurt your other friends. You need to calm down so we can find her. There's still time. Listen to my voice and breathe." He continued talking until my fists loosened and my heart slowed. I didn't want them involved in this." I closed my eyes and my voice was barely a whisper in my aching throat.

Cheney leaned his forehead against mine and ran his hand down my hair. "I know." He took a deep breath. "We'll get her back. I promise."

"You can't know that."

"I told you. I will never let anyone or anything hurt you—"

I kissed him softly, appreciating his calmness and self-assurance. His words resonated with me and I knew they were true. Cheney would help me fix this, all of this. He stroked the back of my neck and broke the kiss, but he didn't move away. "Selene—" he rasped before kissing me once more and moving back to his seat. "You should read the note." His eyes didn't quite meet mine.

The supple paper trembled in my hand. I blinked away tears and struggled to focus on the scrawling writing. All it said was, "Perhaps this one will mean more than the last."

Guilt and regret pierced me. Michael had died, and now Devin—*Devin!*—was in danger. All because I didn't follow the finger. I didn't play the sick game. Whoever was behind this was right, though. Nothing would stop me from following the clues this time. Immediately. Traps be damned. I wouldn't fail again.

I kept the letter clutched in my fingers and stood up. "Do you need this for anything?"

He leaned back, rubbing his chin. "You can read it?"

"Of course." I frowned. "Why wouldn't I be able to?"

"It isn't English."

I looked again. Sure enough the words were made of odd scrolling symbols that should have been gibberish, but they weren't. I read them all as easily as a sign on the road.

"You've remembered a lot, haven't you?" he asked.

I bit my lip. "I have more important things to do than discuss my memories. The killer is practically taunting me."

Cheney stood. "And why do you think this letter is for you? It was left in my castle, in my office, and if you turn it over, you will see my name on it. Someone is holding your friend to get to me."

I narrowed my eyes. I had the urge to tell him everything and the urge to reveal nothing. "Why would they take Devin to get to you?"

"Everyone knows I love you. They have taken your friend to make me deal with them. I didn't involve myself with Michael's disappearance. It's my fault he is dead." He looked truly regretful. "But why did you assume this was about you? Have you gotten a different letter?"

"There was one at my house with Michael."

"What language?"

I thought back. "English."

"Are you certain?"

"Yeah." Holden and Olivia were able to read it; it had to be English. "Have demands been made?"

"Sit down." He gestured to a chair. I sat. "Were demands made last time?"

"They wanted me to give you the rebel leader for public execution."

Cheney frowned. "I too received a letter regarding Michael. It wanted me to purge the kingdom of half-elf insolence."

"You didn't tell me?" I snapped.

"Not so hasty on the indignation. You didn't tell me either. It seems we both have our fair share of secrets. But there's nothing new in that."

"So both letters wanted the rebels to be killed."

He met my gaze full on. "Or both letters wanted you dead."

"But if you kill me—"

"I kill myself. Yes, I know."

"Another little detail you failed to mention."

He nodded slowly.

"That's why you came back for me, isn't it?"

"I told myself that was why, but it wasn't, no matter what I wanted to believe."

I took a deep breath. I didn't have time to get into this now. We needed to focus on getting Devin back, safe and unharmed. I cleared my throat. "Where's your father being held?"

"My father couldn't have done this."

"How can you be certain?"

"He is under constant watch. I double-checked everything after I received the first letter. It isn't him."

I sighed. "If you don't need the letter for anything, I'm going to see if I can trace it back to the person who wrote it."

"Do you believe me?"

"I don't know what I believe."

"Selene—"

"Cheney, I can't discuss this right now." I folded the paper and slipped it into my pocket. Then I left the room without looking back. I checked with each of the girls, except Katrina, who was in the shower. None of them had the book. Whoever had Devin had the Book of Shadows too. Jessica and Leslie came with me to Devin's room.

We got Devin's brush and worked together and made a circle. Tracking spells were fairly simple, so it should have worked. But the crystal turned black and began to shake.

"Oh, that's not good," Leslie said.

We all covered our heads just as the crystal exploded, showering the room with glittery shards.

"What the hell happened?" Jessica asked.

I shook my head. I'd never had a spell react like that. "I

don't know, but this isn't over. I'll find another way. I promise I will bring Devin home."

FOURTEEN

Sebastian and Sy were standing in the garden, chatting pleasantly, while Femi investigated the body.

"I'm glad you rushed, Selene. It isn't like I had things to do today," Sebastian said without looking at me.

"Devin was taken," Cheney said behind me.

Sebastian's head snapped back. "How? She was in the castle." Sebastian looked more frazzled than I had ever seen him. Apparently my friends had grown on him. "What are you doing to protect the others?"

"Was she in your coven?" Sy asked.

I nodded and swallowed against the lump in my throat. I had to be strong right now, not so human. "She *is* a member of the coven."

"The others each have personal guards assigned to them," Cheney told Sebastian.

"It's not enough." Sebastian made steps toward the castle and Cheney stopped him.

He nodded to the body. "Selene needs your protection."

"Selene doesn't—" Cheney gave him a look. Sebastian's jaw clenched, but he gave a curt nod and turned back to me. "Where's your grandmother's book?"

"It's gone."

"I assume you have another plan?"

Femi stood apart from us, her eyes contracting with interest as she took everything in. I pulled the letter out and waved it in front of Sebastian. "I'm going to try to find the source." I rattled off what I needed and Cheney went inside to get it. I could have used the coven's help, but I didn't want the same thing to happen to the letter that happened to the crystal when we tried to track her—in case our collective amped-up nerves were overcharging what we were trying to do. I read the letter to Sebastian, Sy, and Femi. When I finished I looked over to Sy. "Why are you here?"

"I brought Femi." He patted my shoulder. "How are you?"

"I'll be fine."

I moved away, not knowing who was watching. Whoever took Devin had access to the castle and knew about the church that Cheney took me to. "Why didn't Cheney just do the thing where he pulls stuff out of the air?" I asked Sebastian with a frown. The longer I waited, the more my stomach twisted into knots.

"I doubt he had those particular items in his holding," Sebastian said, but he stared back at the castle too, his eyelid twitching.

I thought back, trying to place what a holding was but came up empty. "What's a holding?"

He sighed. "It's a small room, if you will, in the in between only accessible by a particular person's magic."

"Do I have one?"

Sy shook his head. "You have to be royalty."

"Why?" That hardly seemed fair.

"It's a difference in magical ability," Sy explained. "The

ancient families who rule the different houses have less, let's say, 'snags,' in their lineage. Their magic is stronger."

Femi scoffed. "A.K.A., inbreeding." She winked at me.

"I've seen you do it," I told Sebastian.

"And what does that tell you?"

"You're royalty?"

He nodded.

"Then why do you work for Cheney?"

Sebastian laughed. "I am the advisor to the Erlking. Many would love to be in my position."

Cheney returned with everything I'd asked for. I drew the circle and meditated for a quiet minute, trying to find my center. When peace eased through me, I began the spell, submerging the parchment into the bowl of water, along with the large, clear crystal. I poured energy into the crystal until I was woozy. Then I broke the circle and clutched a rock in my hands, focusing. A throbbing energy pulled me directly to Sebastian.

I stared at him, my mouth open slightly, and he stared back. That couldn't be right. I moved around him and the energy directed me back to him. I tried again, moving farther away, yet I had the same result. "You. *You* wrote the letter."

His eyes widened and he shook his head.

Sound roared in my ears. Sebastian. No one moved. They stared at us, waiting to see what would happen.

"Selene—"

I slapped him, hard. "How could you? Where is she?"

"I didn't."

"Where is she?" I shouted. My hand twitched, wanting to lash out at him again. I trusted Sebastian, possibly more than I did Cheney, though I couldn't say why. Why would he kill Michael? Why would he take Devin? I wanted to hurt him. A voice in my head reminded me I could hurt him. I tightened my fist, envisioning his lungs constricting with the motion. He grabbed his throat. His face went from pink to purple and headed toward blue.

"What's happening? I heard you were looking for me." Katrina appeared in my peripheral vision. "Oh my god, Sebastian!" She rushed toward him and I snapped out of my rage, releasing him.

My legs gave out and I fell to the ground. Sebastian gasped for air.

Cheney gently moved Katrina to the side, slapped shackles on Sebastian's arms, and handed him to a guard I didn't even see approaching. "Where do you think you're taking him? I have questions for him," I said.

Cheney spoke in a calm, soothing voice. "You're too emotional at the moment, Selene. You'll kill him if I allow you to continue. You won't find out anything if he is dead."

I glared at him. I was in control now. I wasn't going to injure him, not until I knew everything.

"Selene," Sy said in that way of his that sounded oh-so-reasonable—totally infuriating. He was taking Cheney's side.

"Selene, what's happening?" Katrina asked, kneeling in front of me with a tear-streaked face. "Is that Michael? What did Sebastian do?"

My eyes welled with tears. I transported back to the Office and stalked through the bar, past a stoic looking Sy standing in his normal spot behind the bar. How had he beaten me there? I stared straight ahead and marched into the apartment. I crashed onto the couch, burying my face in the pillow, and cried. I cried because Michael had been killed because of me and there was nothing I could do to reverse it. I cried because Devin was gone and I didn't know if I could get her back or even where to begin. And I cried because I was on a pity parade. Finally I rubbed the tears from my eyes, admonishing myself for being weak. I couldn't break down. People were depending on me. I pushed myself up and took several deep breaths.

"Well, that didn't last long," Olivia's voice came from the chair.

I looked over, not believing she was here. "Have you been here the whole time?"

She gave me a sympathetic smile. "Femi thought you might want to talk to someone. Sounds like you had a shitty day."

I chuckled, wiping the remaining tears. "Are your people supposed to cuss?"

She winked. "Holden's a bad influence."

"Michael's dead and one of my best friends is missing," I sniffled.

She nodded. "What are we going to do about that?"

"We're going to find who's doing this." It was just a matter of how. I didn't want to wait for a finger to arrive to start looking.

"Maybe Holden saw something at the ruin this morning?"

I wanted to slap my forehead. It never even occurred to me. "Oh no. He could be hurt. I forgot he was there." I stood up, ready to go.

Olivia stood too. "Holden is fine. It's sweet of you to worry. Let me get Sy and we'll meet him at the church." She calmly walked out of the room and I immediately felt tense again. Something about her presence was settling. She made me believe things would work out okay. Were all guardians like her? Sy followed her back into the room.

"So how do we get there?" Olivia asked.

"I don't think I can explain it. Cheney took me there once. It's an old ruin where his sister and her human lover used to meet, or something like that. He said it's been forgotten by the elves and hidden from the humans. Have you heard of it?" I looked at Sy.

He leaned his head back. "Can't say I have—but you're strong enough to take us all." They each took one of my hands and I focused on the spell and my will. Moments later were standing in the plush glass.

Olivia walked a few steps and looked around, taking a deep breath. "It's lovely here."

"And private." Cheney's voice came from behind us. He frowned at me when I turned around. A moment later Holden formed next to Olivia, as if he'd felt her arrive. "What are they doing here, Selene?"

"Helping me look for Devin."

"And why would she be here?" His voice was soft and too controlled.

"This is where I found Michael." I met his gaze. "Has Sebastian said anything?" Cheney shook his head, but guilt marred his smooth face. "You haven't asked him, have you?"

"He is my friend." Cheney ran his hand through his hair. "I've known him longer than I've known you. I came to think before I made any decisions. And what do you mean this is where you found Michael?"

Holden pointed to the ruin. "He was on the other side of the altar, lots of blood, no heart."

Cheney frowned. "That's not possible."

We went into the church. Holden, Olivia, and Sy trailed behind Cheney and me. I watched him out of the corner of my eye, but his furious jaw was set. Why was he so angry? I almost gasped in relief. The pools of blood had dried to a crusty brown substance, caking the floor, but Devin hadn't taken Michael's place. I bit my lip so I had something to focus on other than emotion. Cheney looked at me.

"And you knew about this before we found him in the garden?"

"Yes." We stared at each other for a long time.

"I keep believing you will stop lying to me, but you never do." Cheney blinked out, and I was left looking at nothing.

I cleared my throat and pressed my lips into a hard line before turning to the others. Holden looked bored, and Olivia smiled at me sympathetically.

"Now what?" Holden asked.

"Now." I thought about it. "Now I am going to see my grandmother." They gave me perplexed looks.

"Why?" Sy asked.

"It was Gram's Book of Shadows. Maybe she knows the spell I will need or at least be willing to help me find Devin."

"Do you still want to meet Baker tonight?" Holden asked and Olivia's mouth fell open.

"Meet Baker about what?"

Holden took her hand, making her glow. "He knows a hoodoo priestess who might be able to break the bond."

Olivia looked back at me. "I wouldn't rush into anything just yet."

I sighed. "I don't know. I'll keep you posted." I glanced

over at Sy. "Please tell Jaron I can't meet him tonight."

Sy nodded and transported out. Holden faded into his thick black smoke, and Olivia grew into a ball of beautiful white light. I took a deep breath and went to the one person who could maybe help me.

FIFTEEN

Gram's green-shingled house with its wraparound porch was as it always had been, but somehow it looked different. I stood outside in the pouring rain, trying to figure out what had changed about it. I wasn't trying to stall about seeing Grandma again. Nope, not at all. The door opened and Grandma walked out, broom in hand. Finally she nodded.

"Come inside," she commanded and turned on her heel. I, as ever when it came to Gram, obeyed. She looked back over her shoulder. "What brings you here?"

"You look good, Gram." It hadn't been just the two of us in a long time. I wished the situation between us was different.

She gave me a cold stare, rejecting my niceties. "Sit," she said.

I sat on a stool in the kitchen, and she poured me a cup of coffee, keeping a wary eye locked on me at all times. "Why are you here?"

I struggled not to roll my eyes. "Why? Can't I just come to visit my grandmother? Why do you hate me now?"

"I don't hate you, Selene. But I know you. You aren't here for just a visit. I see you making bad decisions, and you won't listen to me. You'll kill someone again, mark my words. You're dangerous and need to be controlled. Cheney knows that. But what do I know? I'm just a human …"

"What do you mean, kill someone again? Who did I kill? When?"

She leaned against the counter. "Still can't remember. It's the strangest thing." Her brown eyes pierced into me.

"Please. For the love of God, someone needs to tell me something."

"I suppose there's no harm telling you now." She sipped her coffee. "You killed your parents. Do you still not remember the night you came to live with me?"

My limbs lost all ability to move. I stared at her. I was just a child. How did I kill them? I remembered some of that night, but not all of it. "I remember standing in the house while it fell apart around me. I remember Cheney rescuing me and giving me to you. That's all I remember."

She nodded. "That was after the accident, but it wasn't really an accident, was it? I had never seen such a cold, removed child. Not a tear came from you! You felt nothing for your poor parents. As soon as Cheney was out of sight, you turned around and didn't utter a single word to me until I took you to your room. When I said goodnight, you said 'What about murder makes the night good, human?'" Gram sat her mug down with shaking hands. "The next morning you seemed like the child you appeared to be and never spoke of it again. But I knew different. I knew what was inside of you and why the prince sent you to me. You needed to be controlled, managed."

I didn't remember any of that. The memories I had of my parents were vague at best, but I always blamed that on how young I was when they died. I thought back to my one memory of that night. I had recognized Cheney when he came in, but I didn't recognize him later. Jaron said I gave him my memories before I became a changeling, but if that were the case I wouldn't have remembered Cheney. I wouldn't have said what I did to Grandma. I lost my memories the night my parents were killed.

"You see. My rules were for your protection. They protected you and me and all those around us. Don't think I don't know about who you were. Cheney told me everything when he asked me to take you in."

"He told you everything?" I said. If I knew anything about Cheney, it was that he never told *anyone* everything.

She puffed up her chest. "I know you were a traitor to your race and left him for the rebels. I know, despite what he thinks, that you were more than likely using him to gain leverage in your revolution. I've had many years to think about this, Selene. I've watched you. You are careful, very careful. You manipulate and lead people where you want them to go while letting them think it's their idea to begin with. The only thing I could never figure out is why you suppressed your memories that night ..." She took another long sip of her coffee. "Maybe something inside of you knew that you were a danger." She shook her head. "The truth is, I just don't know what you're capable of now."

I had no idea what to say. I wished I could argue with her, but I had no ground to stand on. I couldn't remember what happened, and no one who could was talking except her. "So you think I killed my parents and have been manipulating Cheney this entire time?"

She nodded. "He's clearly in love with you, and you're

just as clearly *not* in love with him. I have yet to see you moved, child. You are so shut off."

I blinked away tears. "You're right. I used Cheney before I became a changeling. I don't know if I loved him or not, but I definitely had ulterior motives from the beginning."

She nodded. "That's why you shouldn't have gone back with him. You will only hurt him—and that is not a man used to losing. I don't know what he'll do to you when he learns he can never have your heart."

I frowned. I wouldn't go so far as saying *never*. "I'm going to break the bond. That's the only way I can know for certain how I feel about him."

The cup clanged as she slammed it on the hard counter. "Is that why you came?"

"No." I explained about Michael and Devin. Gram listened without commenting until I mentioned the little detail that Devin had the book.

"You lost my book? The only thing I told you to do was protect the book, and you let it slip through your fingers?"

I stood up. "You knew as well as I did that the girls were studying it. How was I supposed to know Devin would be taken from the castle? Besides, what can elves do with human magic?"

"You're assuming an elf took her and not one of your former partners. Half-elves can do quite a lot."

I shook my head. "The spell I used on the letter led to Sebastian."

"Sebastian?" Gram's gray eyebrows nearly blended into her hairline. "I don't think so."

"It did."

"Hmph. Wait here." Gram scurried away and returned a

moment later with an aged-looking sheet of paper. "This is a page from the book. I kept a few hidden so I could always track it in case of an emergency." She held it out. "Find your friend and put an end to this, once and for all."

SIXTEEN

I left Grandma's house with the parchment in hand. I couldn't go alone, but who could I take with me? I could go back and get Sy, but I didn't want him to get hurt. I could no longer trust Jaron; his version of events already had holes in it. I could ask Femi, but I didn't really want to. There was only one person I wanted with me for this. We still had a lot to talk about, but if I knew nothing else, I knew that Cheney would keep me alive even if he was furious with me.

I found him pacing the castle hallways, his face set in a stern line. As soon as he saw me, he grabbed my arm and dragged me into the nearest room, breathing hard.

He started to speak several times but kept stopping himself. His fingers dug into my flesh. Then he crushed his lips to mine. Not gentle, not coaxing, but angry and demanding. I kissed him back and reached for him, but he fought my gentleness and kept me at arm's distance. When he broke the kiss, his eyes stayed closed.

"I thought you would be different this time. I truly believed you loved me underneath everything else. When it was just me and you in the house after I first came to get you, you did, didn't you? It's your memories that are taking you away from me."

My voice shook, but I couldn't completely deny his accusation. "The more I find that you kept from me, the harder it is to trust you. I doubt every feeling I have and it's driving me crazy. Everyone keeps telling me how unfeeling I am, but I don't think I am. I have so many emotions running though me that I can't decipher them all."

He released me and shook his head. "I locked up my best friend, my only friend, without even talking to him on your word. Do you understand what I will have to do to Sebastian to make him talk if he doesn't want to tell me anything? I can't keep doing this, Selene."

I opened my mouth and shut it, trying not to picture the terrible things he could possibly do. Finally I shook it off. "You might not have to do anything," I said. I held up the paper. "I went to see Gram. She gave me a page from the book. We can find it, and hopefully Devin will be there too." I licked my lips. "I thought of all the people I could take with me to do this and you were the only one I wanted."

"Why?"

"I'm not sure about these memories anymore. I was told I gave my memories away before I became a changeling, but I recognized you when you came the night I killed my parents." The words were hard to say and almost got lodged in my throat. I was a murderer.

Cheney's mouth fell open. "The night you *what*?"

I shook my head. "Gram told me."

"That you killed your parents?"

I swallowed back tears.

"You didn't kill anyone. I suspected it wasn't an accident that killed them, but it wasn't you either. I would've recognized the magic. That's why I had her cast wards on you, to protect you from whoever came for you that night. I never imagined she would so completely misunderstand."

My knees felt weak so I braced myself against the chair. "Are you telling me the truth?" My voice cracked as I spoke.

Cheney took my hands. "Every word."

Tears slipped out. "What about my memory?"

"I have no idea what happened to it. You said you recognized me, so you lost it sometime after that."

"Gram said I was a normal little kid by morning, so something happened between the time I got to her house and the next morning."

He shook his head. "I'm sorry. I should've stayed with you like you asked."

I pressed a finger to his lips. "Shh." I had to trust someone. I took a deep breath and pushed through before I could change my mind. "I don't remember Sebastian at all. I have a lot of my memories back, but for some reason, he's nowhere in them."

Cheney pulled me over to a couch. "That doesn't make sense."

"I know. I'm going to tell you everything I remember. I need you to tell me if you remember anything differently, but we can't do it right now. Right now we need to find Devin before she turns up like Michael."

He looked at the paper then back to me. "And if we can't find her?"

"I will give you the rebel leader."

He shook his head. "I don't want you to."

My eyes welled again.

He gave me a sad smile. "You know I loved you from

the first moment I saw you. I didn't care what my family thought. You were all I ever wanted. I didn't need a bond to assure that I would come after you, Selene. I would always come for you." He let out a slow breath. "We bonded to bring you back from something terrible that happened to you. I almost lost you. Your mind was nearly shattered, so I became your anchor. I don't know what breaking the bond now would do to you."

I could actually remember the first time we met. How cold and calculated I was on the inside. Did I feel anything for him then? It was so hard to remember. Jaron eclipsed all of my feelings back then. I did remember, however, how I felt the first time we kissed when he came for me as a changeling. All of that couldn't have been mere magic. "What happened?"

He brushed the back of his hand down my cheek. "You'll remember soon enough, and I will be here."

I didn't like that he still refused to tell me, but it wasn't important at the moment. "Will you help me find Devin?"

"Of course."

We quickly laid out the necessary components for the spell. Minutes later we were following a trail, hand in hand. It led us back to the ruin. "Why are we here?"

I shrugged. "I followed the crystal." I walked back inside.

"But we were just here. You would have—"

We saw the book smack-dab in the center of the altar, waiting for us. I approached it warily and tapped it with my finger twice to make sure nothing horrible was going to happen. I picked up the heavy book, and a letter fell out. Cheney stooped to pick it up.

"I'm glad to see I have your attention," he read out loud. He looked at me. "That's it. That's all it says."

"Gah!" I yelled. "How is the person always one step ahead of me? It's like I'm a puppet and someone else is the puppeteer."

"We'll find her, princess." He wrapped his arms around me.

It had been a long time since Cheney called me princess. I'd missed it a little. I leaned into him, needing his reassurance. We were back to square one. No leads. No hope. "Baker found someone who can break the bond," I said.

"I told you—"

"I know. But we need to talk to this lady to know what options we have."

Cheney sighed. "Only if you tell me everything before we go. No more surprises."

"Fine, but it isn't fair that I tell you everything and you still tell me nothing."

"You're right. I'll fill in whatever blanks I can. But I want everything, including the rebel leader."

My heart stuttered. "I thought you didn't want him."

He shook his head. "I don't want to execute him, but I do want to know who he is."

We sat against the cool stone wall, and I started at the beginning. Cheney listened quietly, watching my face as I spoke. I did as promised. I didn't leave out details, no matter how painful they were to tell. His eyes darkened as I spoke about Jaron, but he still didn't interrupt. I spoke faster to get to the end sooner so I could find out what he was thinking.

He sighed. "The memories themselves seem fairly accurate. I can't say what happened when I wasn't there or how you felt while I was. I don't know if that's right or not. I would like to think you felt more about me than that, but maybe you didn't." He couldn't hide the hurt from his eyes, but his voice sounded calm, even a little resigned.

I leaned my head back against the wall and closed my eyes, scanning my memory for any glimmer of hope that I wasn't a completely horrible person. I found it right in front of me. It had been there the whole time. The first memories I had were overshadowed in my mind, but they were still there. The ones I didn't connect with—that had been torn from me and regained with agony through spell work—were different than the later ones. I was anything but ambivalent toward Cheney in those. "My other memories were different. I felt different in those."

Cheney looked over at me. Doubt filled his eyes, and who could blame him? I'd been acting psychotic, and I'd just finished telling him I'd never loved him. "How different?"

"Like leaving you was the hardest thing I ever had to do."

He stood up. "So we just have to figure out which one is right." He held out his hand. "Let's go meet Baker."

I took his hand and we transported to the Office. I felt better for having told Cheney everything, though it occurred to me he hadn't upheld his end of the bargain.

SEVENTEEN

Sy was chatting up a pretty redhead when we walked into the Office. I shook my head and hoped Femi would make an honest man out of him someday. If Sy was shocked by Cheney's presence, he did a good job hiding it. He held out his hand. "Nice to see you again."

Cheney shook Sy's hand, his eyes traveling over the bar. "Nice place."

Sy laughed. "No need to spare my feelings. Can I get you a drink?"

We both declined. "So who's your friend?" I asked.

He glanced down to the end of the bar. "Gretchen. She's a muse." He smiled to himself. "Very inspiring."

Cheney laughed and I shook my head. "You know, you're never going to get Femi to go out with you like this."

Sy kissed the top of my head. "Mind your own business, coz."

"Were you guys always this close?" Cheney asked.

Sy shrugged. "We were as kids, but we haven't really seen each other or talked for a while." He winked at me and went back to Gretchen.

"Was it me or Jaron who caused you to give up your

family?"

I had to think about that. Automatically my mind told me it was Cheney, but I couldn't find any memory evidence to support that. I had stopped hanging out with Sy before Cheney was ever in the picture. "Jaron I think."

He nodded. "Are you going to try to get the rest of your memories?" Cheney knew exactly how I had to retrieve my memories, so I knew what he was asking.

"I don't know. I missed the piece of time between when I left the first time and when I became a changeling. I'd like to know what happened then, but if there's another way to find out, I'd be open to that."

"I still can't imagine how Sebastian fits into all of this."

I shook my head. "I trusted him."

"I still do." Cheney looked at me. "None of this adds up. You have to see that."

"You didn't keep your end of the deal. What do you know?"

"Baker's here," Cheney said, avoiding telling me once again.

"Hey, fox." Baker slung his arm over my shoulder. "I see you're back with the big cheese."

"Hey, Baker." I gave him a tight smile. "So who's this priestess?"

"Antoinette Cecile. She's down in New Orleans and is really good with curses and what not. When the boss-man asked me to look into your little problem," his eyes drifted to Cheney, "she was the first person to come to mind. She'll have a price. I don't know what, but nothing's ever free."

I looked at Cheney. "What do you think?"

"Let's see what she has to say."

We stood outside of Winston's Wash and Dry and a red "Open" sign buzzed in the dingy window. I looked at Baker. "This is where we're meeting?"

Strange, drum-heavy music played inside the laundromat, and the handful of people eyed us as we headed toward the "Employees Only" door. Baker walked through without hesitating, and Cheney and I were right behind him.

"Who's there?" an old woman in a dated green dress hissed from her perch on a metal chair. "You're not from the natural world. Hoo boy, we got some power circulating tonight, yes, we do." A mess of bones, charms, and things I couldn't begin to identify were strewn on a small altar next to her.

"Toinette." Baker kissed both of her cheeks. "How have you been?"

She tilted her head toward the sound of his voice, her milky white eyes unfocused and drifting eerily around the room. "Baker, you sly devil, is that you? It's been a score since you carried yourself down here to these parts." She snatched his hand with unerring accuracy. "Hoo, mischief and trouble. Boy, that is all I ever feel in you. But you're not alone this time. Who did you bring?"

"Toinette, these are my friends Selene and Cheney. They—"

"Hush," she told him. "Hands." She held out her thick arthritic fingers. Cheney took one hand and Baker nodded at me encouragingly. I squeezed my hand into a loose fist and placed it in her waiting grasp.

Her breath whistled, and she released Cheney and gripped my wrist with her other hand, pulling me closer. "So much magic. So many spells and curses on one little girl." She ran her hand up and down my forearm. I tried to pull away, but her grip was strong—too strong. "So much confusion. You can't see up from down."

Her head lulled back and she began to cough, releasing my hand. "I can't help you. Leave."

"Toinette—"

"Take them away, Baker."

He frowned down at the old woman. "I've known you a long time and you've never been a piker. You owe me," he said.

She stood up, wringing her hands, her metal chair falling to the side. "You do not know what you ask."

"We haven't asked for anything yet," I said.

"You're trouble. Too much trouble." She wagged a finger at me. I looked over at Cheney. He appeared to be holding back a smile. *Great.*

"It's fine. Let's just go. Thank you for your time." I turned to leave, not wanting to admit how much she freaked me out. What was wrong with me?

"Hold up," Baker called. I turned back toward him and he stared at me with a contemplative expression. "Something must be bad wrong with you, doll. But the boss-man said to help and that's what I'm going to do." He looked back at the old woman. "What's eating you, Toinette?"

"You brought all that hate and rage into my office, Baker McGovern. I have half a mind to curse you too."

I shook my head. "I'm not angry."

"Not you, child. The person who did this to you. You're

wrapped like a mummy in powerful curses. I want no part of it."

"Cheney no longer looked amused. "Curses? What kind of curses?"

"The worst kind." Antoinette's unseeing gaze fluttered in my direction. "I feel death, strife, struggle digging their way inside. It won't stop until her heart is as black as the magic that did this."

I shook my head. She wasn't right. The only spells that were cast on me were by my grandmother and coven. They were spells of protection and to help me remember. "No. You're wrong. Look, I just want to break the bond with Cheney. Can you tell me how to do that?"

She came toward me and took my hand again. I didn't know how she knew exactly where I was, but she did. After a moment, she spoke. "I wouldn't remove that bond for all the riches in the world. It's the only thing keeping you from falling to the darkness. It's your lifeline and even it is weakening."

"Cheney?" I looked at him. He was the only one who knew why we bonded.

He shook his head. "You weren't cursed that I know of. She wasn't cursed."

"Why did you come if you aren't going to listen? The girl is a danger to all those around her."

I took a deep breath. "I'll listen. Please tell me what you know."

She looked through me and nodded once. "Baker, you and the Erlking wait outside."

"I'm not leaving," Cheney said.

"I'll be okay," I told him, and Baker ushered him out of

the room.

"Have a seat, child." Another metal chair appeared in front of her chair. We both sat and she took both of my hands. "This is old magic, older than I have felt on a living person. To withstand it, you must be strong. Now tell Toinette. Why did you come here to break the bond with the elf king?"

I bit my lip. "It's confusing me. I don't know what I feel or think. I can't remember my past very well, but the more I think I know about it, the more confused I get."

"Does it hurt to remember? Cause you pain?"

I nodded.

She shook her head. "Nodding to a blind woman." Her hands moved up my face. "The curse is holding back the memories. It has the power to kill you if you continue to pluck at them."

My mind went back to my conversation with Grandma. What if Cheney was wrong? What if I had killed my parents? Maybe I then cursed myself to keep me from harming anyone else. I could have given my memories to Jaron so I wouldn't lose them completely but bound the power inside of me so I could do no harm. "It's a curse, not a binding. Are you sure about that?"

"This is no binding. It is made from anger and resentment. Strong. I don't know if I can break it, but if you can rid yourself of it, I can undo the bond on the harvest moon."

"That's less than two weeks."

"Don't quote me the time when you do not have it to waste. If you don't end the curse by the moon you will be lost anyway."

"How do I break it?"

"Everything comes with a cost. Are you willing to pay it?"

"What is it?"

"That will be revealed in time. Will you pay it?"

As if I had a choice. It wasn't like I could get a second opinion. The facts were there. I didn't have a memory I could trust. And no matter what I wanted to believe, darkness was surrounding me and hurting those I loved. "I will."

She picked out a handful of items that looked like trash to me, stuffed them into a little burlap bag, and pulled the string tight. "Find the person who cursed you. Soak this in their blood, then in yours, and cast it into a fire made from wood of an ash tree and sage. Make sure you have it right, child. You only have one chance."

"Thank you."

She nodded. "If you succeed, we will meet again."

"And if I don't?"

Her lips pursed. "Then pray for death."

EIGHTEEN

"Death?" Sy wiped the rag over the bar for the hundredth time.

"That's what she said."

"We'll break the curse and rescue your friend."

"But how am I going to know who did it? Even if I get the rest of my memories from Jaron, who's to say I even knew that I was cursed or that the memories are correct. What if they're tainted by this curse? There are already inconsistencies."

Sy poured us each a shot. "You're right. It's impossible. We should give up." He clinked our glasses together and tossed back his drink.

"That's not what I'm saying," I said, toying with the little glass instead of drinking it. "Do you think I killed my parents?"

He shook his head. "There has to be another explanation. My guess is whoever killed your human parents is also the person who killed Michael and took Devin. Chances are that's also the person who put this curse on you. Someone has a serious hate on for you, coz."

"But who? And why?"

"Well, I think we can rule out Cheney. Doing anything that might kill you after you two bonded would be dumb. So who's left? We have his father. Obviously he hates you."

"Cheney says he couldn't possibly be doing this, but he also hasn't told me where he's being held."

"And there's Sebastian. Your spell led to him."

"I have a hard time believing Sebastian is behind any of this. He seems to really like my friends, and he's been so nice to me. What reason could he have for hating me and wanting me dead? He knows it would kill Cheney too."

"Maybe that *is* the reason. Maybe Sebastian is making a play for the crown and he's using you to do it. There's no reason why his house couldn't rule just as easily or as well as Cheney's. Is Sebastian really as loyal as he seems?"

"And there's Jaron," I said, though my mind was still on Sebastian and Sy's interesting point. "Obviously he is involved somehow."

"He did lie about when he got the memories. Are you going to get the rest from him?"

I shrugged. "I don't know. I have this feeling that if I do, I will be choosing Jaron over Cheney."

"If it is the only way to find out, then maybe it's worth it. Save your friend and yourself. Then worry about the guys."

"There might be another way. If I can remember on my own …" I stood up and stretched. "But I don't have to decide anything tonight. I'm going to bed. Tomorrow, I'll make Cheney tell me what he knows and talk to Sebastian."

"Goodnight. I'll let you know if I hear anything from Femi, Holden, or Olivia."

I started for the back. "Sy." He looked over at me. "If

someone is targeting me, it's only a matter of time before they come after you too."

He smiled. "They'll need a hell of a lot more than luck to get to me."

I shook my head. "Watch your back."

"Why? What happened?"

I whirled around to see Jaron standing in the doorway. "What are you doing here?"

He gave me a half smile. "You keep canceling. Believe it or not, this isn't fun for me."

I swallowed. "I'm sorry. I have a lot going on."

Jaron closed the distance between us, and while it appeared Sy was minding his own business, I knew he was watching every move Jaron made. "Which is why I asked what happened."

"My friend Michael was killed and another friend of mine was taken."

He nodded. "Why?"

"I wish I knew. You have any ideas?"

"Maybe. Let's talk." He nodded toward the back room.

I led the way back, tired and not wanting to do this.

"Have I done something to make you mad?"

"No. I'm sorry. I'm tired." We sat in our usual spots. "When did I give you my memories?"

He paused. "Just before you became a changeling."

Still lying. Why? "And why did I become a changeling?"

"You know the answer to that."

"It doesn't make sense. I feel like all of this must be connected, but I can't see how."

He shrugged. "I'd look at the king. Cheney may have

hidden him away somewhere, but he has loyal followers who will do whatever they can to help get rid of you. Maybe it's someone closer to you than you think."

"I'm pretty sure it's not Cheney."

"Perhaps not—but he does have the same advisor as his father though."

Everything in me stilled. "Sebastian was the king's advisor, too?"

"Don't you remember?"

I shook my head, and he frowned. "Odd."

Yes, I thought. Very odd. Very odd indeed.

After looking in all the usual places for Cheney, I headed to gym on the off chance he was planning on meeting me there, even though I didn't have Sebastian to train me anymore. I found him gracefully pacing on the balance beam, his hair unruly and eyes wild. His head snapped up. "You're late." He hopped down and came toward me with long strides. "Did you have any trouble this morning?"

"No. I was here on time. I didn't know where you were."

He ran his hand vigorously through his hair. "I wish you stayed last night."

"I needed to talk to Sy. He's probably a target too, so I wanted to warn him and tell him everything that happened."

Cheney took me by both shoulders and gazed down with earnest eyes. "I don't care if you have to move every person you have ever known in here. I want you where I can get to you."

"You'll never get Sy here. He's attached to the bar." I touched Cheney's cheek, and he released his breath. "But thank you for the offer." I went over to the mats and sat down. "Now tell me what you know."

Cheney sat in front of me. "Are you sure it's a good idea?"

"Damn it, Cheney, you promised."

"I don't care about you remembering it. I don't want to spark another memory. The woman last night said they could kill you."

"Would you rather I go to Jaron?" He frowned and looked down. I waited a moment, but I wasn't feeling particularly patient. "Cheney?"

"I'm considering," he said.

I leaned back, resting my hands on the floor behind me.

"Fine. I'll tell you. You went to see my father without me knowing about it, but luckily Sebastian saw you before you met with him."

The room felt like it was spinning, but I didn't mention it. I didn't want Cheney to stop. I needed to know.

"He tried to talk you out of seeing the king, but you insisted. You said you had information for him, something he had to know."

The room went black, starting at the edges, then fading in. Cheney's voice sounded hollow and far, far away.

I walked through the doors like I belonged there, ignoring the fact that the king hated me. I was vaguely familiar with the castle from the few times Cheney had brought me there. The king wasn't in the great room, so I went through the door to the private chambers where I promptly ran into Sebastian.

His eyebrows pulled together. "Selene? What are you doing here?" He grabbed me by the arm and pulled me toward the door. "Does Cheney know you're here?"

"This has nothing to do with Cheney. I need to see the Erlking. Where is he? I have information he needs, Sebastian."

Sebastian tilted his head and a knowing look spread over his face. "Don't do this. You chose Jaron and that's fine. We'll manage. Don't try to insert yourself again. You will only hurt Cheney." Concern filled his eyes.

"It's not what you think. I'm protecting Cheney. Jaron isn't who you think he is. He doesn't care about our cause, Sebastian. You can't trust him." My eyes filled with tears. Everything I had believed was tainted. I was disillusioned, but I couldn't stop now. I had to make things right.

Sebastian nodded. "I believe you, but you still cannot see the king. He will imprison you, Selene."

"That's absurd." I pulled out of his grasp and headed down the hallway with Sebastian hot on my heels. I opened the first door I heard talking behind, Sebastian's fingers just missing catching the back of my dress.

The Erlking looked over from his finely crafted leather chair, and my father's eyes turned to me from the chair across from him.

I steeled my spine. The speech I had practiced a thousand times in my head was nowhere to be found. "I-uh-I'm leaving." The king looked at me as if I'd lost my mind. I clenched my fists and tried to force out the words I wanted to say. "After today I will no longer be a part of the fae community. I was born a half-elf and lived in the shadows of *your kingdom all of my life. I once naively thought if my father met me, he could love me, but you would never allow that. I thought if I could win the love of your son, you would have to see me and my kind as more than inferior, but you hated us more for my effort. I thought if I could speak to you, I could make you hear, but your ears are deaf to my voice. I cannot change your mind and I no longer have it in my heart to fight against you so I am leaving.*

"But I cannot leave things as they are. I may have been part of the revolution, but I never wanted this. You and Cheney are both in danger—" I was about to tell him they had to stop Jaron, but the king interrupted me.

"That was a fine speech, Selene, but do you know what else it was?"

My eyes met his.

"Treason. And treason is punishable by death. However, death is far too lenient for you. You are sentenced to the pit where you can think about your crimes."

I turned to flee—Sebastian was right. I shouldn't have come—but two guards took me by the arms. I struggled and yanked away from them, but they were unfazed. I bit one and was met with a firm fist in my kidney. I unleashed energy and waited for the room to shake and crumble around us, but at the first tremor, the guard smashed something hard against the back of my head.

When I awoke, the room was blacker than black. Even my sensitive eyes couldn't pick up enough light to give me any sort of bearings. It could have been the size of a closet or the size of a stadium for all I knew. I felt my way to the wall and waited. Sebastian knew I was in here, he had to. He wouldn't let me rot down here.

Days, months, perhaps years passed. I had no concept of time. No one spoke to me, and I never saw any light. I was beaten and brutalized in every possible manner. Time blurred together in misery. I quickly discovered my magic was worse than useless. The room was warded and the door was made of solid iron. Any chance of escaping on my own was gone. I couldn't even protect myself from the guards. I ran over all the mistakes I'd made in my life, all the choices I should have made differently. But eventually even my regret gave way. I had nothing. I was locked away, forgotten in a dark, empty room with no contact other than to receive pain and nothing but my thoughts, rats, and whoever came down to my cell to fight off. My mind weakened and cracked until Selene died and only anger existed. I no longer cared why Jaron was doing it. He was right. The king had to die.

Hands gripped my shoulders and pulled me off the floor and out of my own squalor. I fought like a wild animal, the animal the king had turned me into, and I hated him. That was the only piece of me left—a burning, consuming rage toward the Erlking. He would die, and he would die by my hands. I clawed and growled at the person trying to take me from my cell as if I could get to the king through him. My fingernails sank deep into his flesh, but still he said nothing. What new, horrible punishment had the king dreamed up this time? A hand covered my mouth and I bit at it, but it only pressed tighter as I was carried from my dark seclusion. The night sky seemed so bright that my eyes watered, and I squeezed my eyelids shut. I didn't want to see the moon if it would be taken away from me again.

A moment later I was released. My legs gave out and I landed in a heap on the floor. I tried to see where I was, but the light was too bright. Tears streamed from my eyes. I curled into a ball. A soft hand brushed my hair back from my face. "It's okay," the familiar voice whispered. "I have you. You're okay."

The following days were a blur. As long as no one touched me, I lay on the couch quietly, drifting in and out of consciousness. Bits of conversations drifted into my thoughts.

"You want to bond with her? Cheney, have you lost your mind?"

"It's the only way. It will bring Selene back."

"She left you."

"She came back, Sebastian."

"She won't even let you touch her. How do you plan on bonding with her?"

"She's getting better. Watch." A hand ran down my cheek. I flinched away but didn't attack him.

"This is a waste of time." Hands grabbed me and jerked up. My eyes opened, no longer sensitive to the light. My fists beat against the man with short brown hair and silvery skin. "Are you mad, Selene? Good and mad," he yelled in my face as I hit him.

"Then fight back. Save yourself." Sebastian took a swing at me and I blocked him, parts of my mind slipping back into place. "No one can break you unless you let them."

"I'll kill him," I growled, lunging for a sword.

"No, you don't." Cheney wrapped an arm around my waist, holding me back.

"Let. Go."

Sebastian stepped in front of me. "This isn't the way, Selene."

They spent hours talking at me. Cheney tried to convince

me to bond with him and Sebastian argued against it. I didn't care what they said. I knew exactly what I was going to do. I wasn't going to hurt Cheney, but the King had to go. I considered telling Cheney what I knew about Jaron, but I didn't do it. It would only strengthen the King's position, and I had Cheney where I needed him. I knew what I had to do. It was the only way to fix this.

When I was strong enough, I transported to Jaron. Shocked doused his face and he stood. "I thought you were dead."

"I'll do it. I'll become a changeling."

A slow smile spread over his face. "You see that I was right all along, don't you? Your peaceful solutions will never work, not with people like that."

I nodded. "I do."

"You'll kill the king and his son? No deviations, Selene."

I swallowed. "Yes."

"If you fail again or get in my way..." He didn't have to finish the threat. I knew what he would do.

"I won't fail."

"We'll perform the ceremony tomorrow."

I walked through the rain one last time, the cold drops pelting against my skin. I wasn't going to hurt Cheney. Despite everything Jaron had drilled into me, he wasn't my enemy. I fought against the darkness inside of me and didn't allow myself to forget the good. If I were being honest, I loved him. My time imprisoned taught me one thing. When I was alone and aching and hurt, I didn't think about Jaron coming to rescue me. It was always Cheney on my mind. I would sooner die than hurt him and there was only one way to make sure that happened. I banged my fist against Cheney's door. He opened it, wearing worn jeans and nothing else. He leaned his forearm against the frame and gave me a crooked smile.

"I knew you'd come back."

"I'll do the bond, but only under one condition."

He stood back, letting me inside, softly shutting the door behind me. "You have conditions?"

I faced him full on, water dripping from my hair onto his floor. "Make me into a changeling."

He shook his head. "What? Why?"

I concocted a story he would believe about the rebels needing me to do it for power. It was true in a way. I told Cheney what I needed to, produced tears in all the right places, until he bent to my will. He tried to talk me out of it, describing how I would have to be sacrificed on an altar and the magic required, but I was unmoved. He said he didn't have the power to do what I was asking, but I knew if he put his mind to it, we would find a way.

"It has to be tonight or I am going to run, and this time, I'm not coming back."

Cheney agreed. I was a wedding and an execution away from the beginning of the end.

Killing the Erlking and Jaron was the only thing that mattered. It would fix everything that was wrong. And if all went well, Cheney would never need to know.

NINETEEN

"Wake up, Selene. Wake up." Cheney's persistent voice kept after me.

"It's not working," Sy said.

"You think I don't know that?" Cheney snapped. "Selene, love, open your eyes."

I peeled back one eyelid to look at him so he'd stop shaking me so hard my brain rattled. He crushed me into a hug. "I thought you were dying. Are you okay?"

My mouth was dry and pasty. "It was just a memory, don't flip out. Happens all the time." I fell limp against him. At least I wasn't bleeding.

"It wasn't 'just' a memory. You had a seizure and nearly scared the crap out of the Erlking," Sy said, and I could hear the smile in his voice, but hearing "Erlking" made me remember.

"I remember what happened. I remember why I became a changeling."

"I really don't care," Cheney said into my shoulder.

I started to tell Cheney everything, but I stopped. I needed to think about it. I needed to talk to someone who knew a lot more than he let on. "I want to see Sebastian."

"Why? Does he have something to do with this?" Cheney asked.

"Maybe. I need to see him. Alone." An annoyed, stubborn look I knew too well started to form on Cheney's face. "Trust me. I will tell you everything."

"If I get a vote—and I think I should as her only family present—I say no," Sy said. "You don't want her to have another memory in the dungeon with no one there to help."

"Sy has a point."

I forced my legs to move and stood up, though my muscles screamed in protest. "I guess I should have said, 'I'm going to see Sebastian alone.'" I walked a couple steps before a wave of dizziness hit me and I stumbled. Cheney caught me, moving me to a chair.

"I don't trust you. Why? Why do you need to see Sebastian?" he asked, standing over me.

I didn't want to tell Cheney that Sebastian had been working with me, though I was pretty certain that was the case. I wanted to talk to him and have him fill in some gaps. Then we could decide how to let Cheney know the depth of our deceit. "I think I told him more back then than he has let on. I want to confirm a few things I suspect but don't know yet."

"And what does this have to do with the curse? With Devin?"

I frowned. "I don't know. Maybe nothing. Maybe something. I need to talk to him—and I think he'll be more forthcoming with just me."

His breath huffed out. "Selene."

"Cheney." I gave him my own stubborn glare.

He rolled his eyes. "Do you think he had anything to do

with Michael or Devin?"

I thought about it. "There's only one way to find out."

Cheney looked back at Sy who shrugged. "Let me have him brought up to you. I don't want any memories sparked by going down there."

"It's okay. I've already remembered that."

All firmness melted from his eyes and he knelt in front of me, cradling my face. "I hoped if there was anything you wouldn't remember, it would be that."

"It's okay. You saved me." I ran my thumb over his bottom lip.

"What am I missing? When was Selene in the dungeon?" Sy asked.

I stood up and patted sweet Sy on the shoulder. "I'm going now. I feel stronger. Cheney will fill you in." I eased my wobbly legs forward.

"If you aren't back in ten minutes, we're coming to get you."

I nodded. It was time for Sebastian to come clean. I headed for the dungeon, but I was intercepted by Katrina, Leslie, and Jessica.

"Where have you been?" Jessica demanded. "Have you found Devin?"

"I have been trying to find her. I'm sorry I haven't come to update you guys."

Leslie shook her head, eyes glistening. "Don't worry about us. Find her. If you need our help, you know where we are."

I nodded. "Where are your guards?"

"We ditched them."

"They're here to protect you. Don't ditch them."

Jessica threw up her arms. "We can help you. We have powers of our own." She glared at me, and I suddenly understood what Cheney must've felt like half the time we were arguing. I was treating them like ... humans, protecting them for their own good. I hadn't thought about their gifts. Leslie's empathy abilities didn't work with fae, so she couldn't help, but Jessica possibly could. She had a knack for knowing when people were lying. Where I was telekinetic, she was telepathic, and as far as I knew fae weren't immune to it.

"You know, you're right. I think you can help me, Jess."

She raised her eyebrows. "Great, how?"

"Come with me. You two go back to your guards—please."

Katrina looked at me with red-rimmed eyes. "Talk to Sebastian, Selene. It has to be a mistake," she said. "He wouldn't hurt Devin or do *that* to Michael."

Damn it. I had abandoned her right after she saw a dead body. I didn't even think twice about it. I was a terrible friend. I nodded and squeezed her hand. "I'm sorry you saw that. I really have to go though. I promise we'll talk soon."

I caught Jessica up as much as I could as we went down the winding stairs. "Basically, I need you to be my lie detector."

"I can do that." She pushed her red hair behind her ears.

"Don't say anything or ask any questions. I'll answer everything later. We'll only have a couple minutes before Cheney comes down to find me."

The guard at the door led us through to a dim room with a thick wooden table. Moments later Sebastian was brought out. He looked like he always did, as if being confined hadn't affected him at all. His experience was obviously not as traumatic as mine was.

"I hoped it'd be you to come to see me," he said as he sat down. "Jessica, it is nice to see you again."

"Yeah, whatever. Give me your hand," she said briskly.

Sebastian laid his arm in front of her without complaint.

"So you're a rebel. Who would have thought?" I said.

"No one. That's why it was brilliant." He smiled a little. "You have finally remembered me?"

I shook my head. "I've had one memory of you. You're the one who told Cheney where I was when I was the king's prisoner?"

He nodded.

"You tried to help me that day. What else did you do? How else did you help me?"

"I fed you information that gave the rebels the early wins they needed to gain momentum and keep people from getting hurt."

"Why?"

He thought for a moment. "You know, I have wondered that myself several times over the years. You're the one who recruited me, but I don't think it really had anything to do with you. I believe in your cause. I never liked Jaron much, but I understood what you were working toward and respected that. Everyone deserves a place, and the half-elves have been overlooked for too long." Sebastian's posture was relaxed and his face open. "That day you were captured, you said Jaron couldn't be trusted. What did he do?"

"My questions first. Why can't I remember you in the memories Jaron has given me?"

"Jaron is giving you memories?"

"He said I gave them to him before I became a changeling, but I know it couldn't have been before."

"You wouldn't have given your memories to him. That much I can tell you."

"Why not?"

"Because you wouldn't have wanted him to know what you were feeling. You were conflicted, Selene. You're not so different now than you were then. Your feelings for Cheney had grown, matured. They were starting to crack whatever hold Jaron had on you. That's why you left the first time. You couldn't hurt Cheney by killing the Erlking, as was your plan when you first set sight on him. You decided that you would take Jaron up on the offer he always dangled in front of you. For all your talk of equality, you never really wanted to be part of the elves. You couldn't reconcile yourself to the fact that you loved the person you saw as your enemy. So you ran." He shrugged. "You and Jaron were supposed to leave and live a life away from the fae. I honestly thought you could be happy if you gave up your resentment—that maybe everything would return to normal."

"What happened?"

"I have no idea. All I know is you came back and told me Jaron couldn't be trusted. Then you were taken and it took Cheney and me over a month to get to you. When you came out, it was—"

"Yeah, I know."

"Then, by the time you were well enough to explain anything, you decided to become a changeling. The last thing you said to me was, 'Take care of Cheney. He's the future.'"

I nodded and looked at Jessica.

"He's telling the truth," she said.

"Why didn't you tell me any of this?"

"You didn't remember, and I couldn't be sure you were ever going to be the Selene I knew back then again. There was no need to stir up the past if you could slip into place alongside Cheney. I always thought the two of you could make a bigger difference together than apart. He listens to you, and though you don't want to, you listen to him. You always have."

I took a deep breath. "Are you working for the Erlking?"

"Yes."

I bit my lip, not sure what to say.

"But I am not working for his father," Sebastian said gently.

I smiled. I still had trouble thinking of Cheney as the Erlking. "Do you know where Devin is or who killed Michael?"

"No." He gave me a hard stare. "I would never harm your friends."

"What do you know about curses?"

"Nothing."

I looked to Jessica and she nodded. "Why did the spell lead me to you?"

"I honestly have no idea. I can't explain it."

I leaned closer. "I became a changeling to save Cheney. Jaron won't stop until he is dead."

"He wants Cheney dead too? Why?"

"I wish I knew." I glanced back at the door, knowing Cheney would be there any moment. "I think we need to tell him everything."

Sebastian set his jaw. "He will most likely execute me," he shook his head, "but I think you are right."

"He hasn't killed me yet, so maybe you have a chance."

Sebastian didn't look convinced. "I'm not you."

I didn't want to keep anymore secrets. We would just have to make Cheney understand. "We have to tell him."

"Tell me what?" I turned around. Cheney was standing in the doorway.

It was now or never. I ignored the butterflies and let my mind scramble for a plan. "Sebastian didn't kill Michael."

"You are certain?" he asked.

I nodded. "I brought my lie detector with me." Jessica waved at him.

A smile broke across his serious face, and he gave Sebastian a manly hug—the kind with one arm and two hard pats on the back. "I'm glad to have you back, my friend. I was sure you were innocent, but I didn't know how to prove it."

"I figured. Otherwise you would have questioned me."

"And that's what you wanted to tell me?" Cheney said, looking back at me with relief.

"No. But I think we should move out of here to talk about it," I said, buying time. Cheney already knew most of the bad things about me, so I wasn't too worried about that. My intention at the time to kill his father, while terrible, was probably understandable—especially since I didn't do it. Sebastian's involvement though . . . Well, that was another story.

Cheney looked at each of us in turn. "Where's your guard?" he asked Jessica.

She smiled a little. "He must've fallen behind."

Cheney sighed and gave me a look that said I should take care of this. I shrugged. "They don't want to be locked in a room and guarded. They have just as much of a right to be involved as we do. They're grown women and they've proven themselves capable. I think it should be their choice."

He nodded. "Very well. I will send for the others. Sebastian, if you would like to clean up, we can meet in my office in an hour."

Sebastian gave a solemn nod, his eyes never leaving me. I tried to give him a reassuring smile before he left.

"Hold up, Sebastian. I'll go with you to get the girls," Jessica said, catching up with him.

Cheney slipped his arm around my waist and I rested my head on his shoulder. "You going to give me a clue about what we are going to talk about?"

"Everything." I looked around the room, wondering if I'd been there before. "Promise me you'll keep your temper."

He pulled his arm away. "More revelations? Fantastic."

"Well, how about I start with the good news?"

He raised an eyebrow. "There's good news? Why do I find that hard to believe?"

I stepped toward him. "My memories from Jaron . . ."

He nodded at me to continue when I paused.

"They don't appear to be all that accurate."

"Which parts?"

"Maybe all—but definitely the parts about us." I rubbed his chest. "Sebastian said I cared about you. I was conflicted and scared, but the feelings were there."

He rubbed his hand over his jaw. "Hmm."

Not exactly the response I expected, though I understood his hesitation. "It's better than never having liked you, right?"

"Indeed." He brushed a strand of hair from my face.

"Are you moving back to the castle now?"

"Do you want me to?"

He nodded. "More than I should."

I kissed him softly. "You know, we just might make it through this." I smiled.

He winked. "One thing at a time."

We walked the stairs hand in hand. I felt better than I had in weeks. I couldn't say why exactly. Maybe knowing that the bond was my decision helped me keep my mind from constantly struggling against it. Or maybe it was the fact that everything was about to be out in the open. Whatever it was, I felt hopeful for the first time in a long time.

TWENTY

Cheney sat still—too still—tapping a finger to his lips. Sebastian stood by the window, silently awaiting the verdict. The girls studied their hands like they wished I hadn't involved them in this awkwardness, but I needed to be upfront with everyone. We didn't have any more time to waste.

"I know how this all sounds, but I also know that you're not blind to the way your father ruled the kingdom." Cheney's eyes moved to me. "I didn't have to tell you this, but I'm tired of the secrets and not knowing who's working with me or against me. We don't have time to play games. Lives are on the line: Devin's, mine—even yours if I die. Was I wrong to tell you?"

"No," he said stiffly. "Just give me a moment to process."

Sebastian shifted but still didn't speak.

"And this is everything? Nothing else is going to pop up?"

I grimaced. "This is all I know right now. I can't swear I'm not going to learn something else. I still can't remember what happened with Jaron exactly or how I lost my memory."

"Sebastian?"

"She told you everything. My involvement began and ended with Selene."

"And you didn't think to tell me about it sooner?"

"Would you have listened?"

More finger drumming. Cheney abruptly placed his hands on his lap. "Okay, fine. Selene's right. We don't have time to waste. Now where do we go from here?"

"We need to find who cursed me and who has Devin," I said.

"Isn't it the same person?" Katrina said.

"Yeah, Occam's Razor," Leslie said.

"The simplest solution is not necessarily the correct one in this case. The person who cursed me is holding back whatever power I could have. The person who took Devin and Michael obviously wants something from me."

"Have you heard anything else?" Jessica asked.

"We had another note delivered today," Cheney said.

"May I see it?" I asked.

"I don't have it. It must've been enchanted because it disintegrated after I read it."

"What did it say?"

"Pretty much the same thing as all the others."

I chewed my thumbnail. "I was a rebel. Give him *me*."

Cheney shook his head. "Not going to happen."

"Not for real. We could fake it. Do the public execution. Then, once everyone thinks I'm dead, no one will be in danger anymore."

"But then you can never come back," Sebastian said. I looked at him. "You do this and you can never return. The elves already aren't sure about you. They won't give you a third chance."

Cheney wore an expression I couldn't read. Finally he blinked and shook his head. "No."

"I'm not going to hide in here and let Devin be killed if I can stop it. If being exiled is the only way, fine. I became a changeling so I could fix things, not make them worse."

"We'll find another way," Cheney said.

"He's right, Selene. You have to at least look for another solution. Devin wouldn't want you to destroy your life," Katrina said.

I wasn't sure that I would be destroying it. If I could claim my elf half, surely I could do the opposite and reclaim my human side once I broke the bond with Cheney. Everything would go back to how it had been. It wasn't ideal, but I could do it. I could live with that solution. "I'm not hearing any other suggestions."

"Let's give them Jaron," Jessica said. "He would be just as good as you."

Cheney lifted an eyebrow and I looked down. I didn't like the idea of trading one life for another. How was it fair to save Devin by killing Jaron? It was different with me; it was my choice. "Do you mean fake his death?"

"Sure, if that's what you want." Jessica shrugged and Leslie slapped her arm. "What? I don't even know him," she said.

"I don't think he'd do it," I said. "But I can ask."

"Fine," Cheney said. "How about the curse?"

He was acting strange, but given everything we'd dumped on him, it was amazing he could stand being in the room with any of us right now.

"Yes, I finally have an idea about that," I said.

Cheney's eyes showed the first real spark of interest they'd had in a bit. "What's that?"

"If my grandmother thought I was a killer, how far would she go to keep me from hurting someone else? Doesn't this seem like something she would do to protect the world from me?"

Cheney rested his ankle on his knee. "Edith is definitely a thought. Why don't you girls go to see her in the morning? Sebastian and I will work on finding Devin. But, for tonight, everyone needs to rest. Don't talk about what we discussed. The less people who know the better." He looked around. "It's been a long day."

The girls went back to their rooms and Sebastian followed them out, leaving me and Cheney alone. "You considered it," I said.

He poured himself a drink. "Considered what?"

"Letting me fake my death and leave."

He tiredly raised a hand. "You volunteered."

"I know." I sat on his lap. "You've been taking care of all of us. I don't think I've asked you if you're okay."

"I'll be fine," he said, trailing his hand down my cheek. "Why are you so caught up with the past? The only feelings that really matter are the ones you have right now."

"That's what everyone keeps telling me."

"And right now, what do you feel?"

What did I feel? That was a good question. "Like I'm finally starting to put pieces together—and that I used to be focused on all the wrong things."

"What are the right things?"

"You and Sy and my friends. None of the rest of it

matters. You guys are all I need to be happy."

"Do you mean it?" His fingers kneaded the muscles in my neck.

"Of course."

"You aren't going to change your mind tomorrow morning?"

I smiled. "I deserve that." I looked into his liquid gold eyes and I knew it deep in the part of me that was only at peace when I was with him. "I love you." The words came out in barely a whisper and I had the urge to look away. I felt bare and exposed as he gazed at me.

He cradled my face in his hands, smiling. "It only took a few decades."

"Maybe after a few more I'll get better at saying it."

"Practice makes perfect." His lips crushed into mine and I matched his force. His tongue flicked out and traced my bottom lip. His hand ran up and down my spine. "I've missed you," I said and slid my tongue over his ear.

His breath hissed out as he lifted my shirt over my head and tossed it to the side. We kissed again, unable to bear the lack of contact for long as I impatiently undid the buttons on his shirt. Once the pesky garment was out of the way, I splayed my hands over his hard chest and pushed back. He looked up at me with hooded eyes. "I'm sorry I told you to go."

"I'm sorry I kept things from you."

"It doesn't matter." His mouth left a hot trail down my neck. My head lulled back, and he slipped the straps of my bra over my shoulders. His tongue dipped into hollow of my neck and traced the sharp edges of my collarbone. I ran my fingernails across his shoulders, taking the tip of his ear in my mouth.

He groaned and stood up. I tightened my legs around him to keep from slipping. He sat me on the desk and feathered kisses across my cheeks, nose, eyelids, and jaw line. The loving tenderness in his touch made my heart swell. "I love you and I wouldn't change a thing that has happened between us. You are perfect, flaws and all," he whispered.

"I love you too." It was easier to say this time. Less frightening, less like it was trapping me, and more like I was finally being set free. I kissed his chest over his heart and drew his flat nipple into my mouth. Cheney's hands went to my pants. Moments later I was bare, and my entire body was throbbing and aching. He left me for a second though—picked up my shirt from where it had landed on the desk.

"You aren't attached to this, are you?"

"What?"

There was a tearing sound.

"What are you doing?" I asked.

"Trust me." He tied the strip of shirt over my eyes, leaving me blind, and laid me back on the desk. "You think too much." A velvet caress started just below my ear and traveled down the length of my body. "Sometimes you just have to feel." His fingers laced with mine and he moved my arms above my head. Then he touched, tasted, and stimulated my body to the point that my skin sizzled with need. He pulled my hips nearer to the edge of the table, and I bit my lip in anticipation. His fingers, one by one, pressed into the flesh of my thighs and I moaned in sweet, sweet agony. "Cheney, please."

He entered me just as slowly, making me feel every inch until we were completely joined. He continued at this excruciating pace, not letting me touch him, making me only feel. Finally, he pulled the blindfold from my eyes. "Hold on to me."

My arms and legs were around him before he even finished his sentence. We moved in harmony, our eyes locked to one another until my vision blurred and I dug my fingernails into his skin. Cheney moved faster and harder, pushing both of us over the edge. He crushed me to his chest and kissed my hair over and over again. "We should probably go to our room," he said.

"Mmmhmm."

Cheney let me go and collected the clothes strewn about the study.

"What am I supposed to wear back to the room?" I said with a laugh, looking at my ruined shirt.

Cheney gave me his shirt and another lingering kiss—and my stomach growled. He grinned. "When's the last time you ate?"

"Who has time for eating?"

He shook his head. "I'll get you something and meet you back in our room."

I pulled him in for another kiss before I let him go. I strolled back to our room and texted Sy that I wasn't coming back to the bar tonight and entered the hash tag "team Cheney." Our room looked completely untouched since the last time I'd been in it. I curled up on the bed to wait for him, but as soon as my head hit the pillow, sleep claimed me. It was good to be home.

TWENTY ONE

I awoke with Cheney's arms around me. The past wasn't going to stand in our way anymore. I was done worrying about it. We would find Devin, break the curse, then get rid of the bond and start fresh.

"You awake?" Cheney said softly, his breath tickling my neck.

"Good morning." I wiggled back closer to him.

He pressed a kiss to the tender spot just behind my ear. I turned and wrapped my arms behind his neck, kissing him slow and deep.

I pulled away a little. "What time is it?"

"Nearly 9:00 a.m."

"Holy smokes, we slept late." I snuck in one more kiss. "We need to get ready. Lots to do." I started to get up and he pulled me back down.

"Just a few more minutes," he said, holding me to him.

I laughed. "You don't even sleep. I'm surprised you're still here."

"I wanted to wake up with you." There was something off in his voice. Something I couldn't quite place.

I twisted so I could see him. "What's wrong?"

He gave me a faint smile. "Nothing. I just missed you."

I snuggled back down. I could get used to this. "I'll call Femi and see if she has any leads."

"I have some things I need to do tonight, so I might be a bit late getting back. Don't worry about me." Again his voice was flat. I rolled over to face him, tucking my hands between my cheek and the pillow.

"Like what?"

"Some last minute details on getting the council off the ground. All the invitations are out and every sub-race has appointed a representative. The council will convene soon. I want to make sure everything goes smoothly."

"What are you going to do about the rebels?" I caught my lower lip between my teeth as I waited for his reply.

He sighed. "We're going to let it go. If you talk to them and they agree to disburse, there is no need to pursue it. I want all of this behind us." He brushed his thumb over the line of worry between my eyebrows. "Did I tell you, your cousin agreed to be on the council, representing the half-elves?"

"Really?" I smiled. Sy getting involved in politics. I'd never thought I'd see the day.

"I hope I'm able to get to know him better."

"Why wouldn't you?"

His eyes drifted to the side. "As an elf you get this feeling of immortality. It is hard to think there might not be time for everything we want to do in this life, but I'm not taking anything for granted anymore. We never know what instant may arise that will change everything we thought we understood."

Was he still brooding over yesterday? I knew finding out

about Sebastian would be a betrayal, but I hoped he would also see that it was a betrayal of his father, not him. But perhaps I was splitting hairs. Or maybe he was worried I wouldn't be able to break the curse. "You know that Sebastian is and has always been loyal to you, right? And we will break the curse."

"Not as loyal as he is to you." Cheney's eyes sparkled at me as a real smile spread across his face. "But I don't mind. I'm glad I can trust him to protect you."

"He never said a word to me about my past because you told him not to."

"In retrospect, getting everything out in the open sooner probably would have been better."

"So you're saying you were wrong . . ."

He kissed me. "Yes."

"And we won't have any more secrets from each other."

The smile melted from his face and seriousness hijacked his eyes. "Not after today." I frowned and was about to ask him to clarify when he climbed out of bed. "No more talk. We have to get dressed. Let's hit the showers."

I wore black leggings and Cheney's button down shirt with a belt. I wanted to keep something of him close to me so I wouldn't forget my resolve once I was away from him. I got the burlap pouch the priestess gave me and attached it to my belt. Not the height of fashion, but at least I wouldn't lose it. The girls and I went to my grandmother's house. I wasn't quite sure how to ask her if she'd cursed me to protect the world, but I had to find out. My friends all looked less emotional and more stable today. Their faces were serious and they were quiet. We walked side by side up the porch, and I knocked on the door before opening it.

"Hello," I called.

Grandma came out of the kitchen with a wooden spoon in her hand. "Did you find the book?" she asked.

I nodded. "But not Devin."

"And you tried a tracking spell?"

"It was blocked," Leslie said. "Everything we have tried has been blocked. We tried to release Selene's memories and failed. We tried to find Devin and failed."

"You know, before we came here and met you, I don't remember a spell of ours ever failing," Katrina said.

"Maybe you're just not strong enough." Grandma turned back to the kitchen.

"Or maybe you've been meddling with our powers," Jessica told her.

I looked at them. "Did you guys plan this?"

"We talked about it last night. It's the only thing that makes sense," Katrina whispered.

I led the way into the kitchen, but Grandma was gone. "Where is sh—" A surge of energy hit my back, knocking me into the stove.

"You've fooled them, but you don't fool me," she said behind me. "I should've taken care of this before we got to this point. I thought maybe you could be saved." Crackling energy formed in her palms and sparks shot out.

"I didn't kill anyone, you crazy old woman."

"You did. I know it. He told me."

"*Who* told you?"

"Cheney." Sparks cascaded around her hand. "He came back to the house the night I picked you up, after you went to bed. He told me everything that happened."

"No." I shook my head. "He spoke with you, but Cheney told me I didn't do it."

"He was clear enough at the time. He is protecting your feelings now."

Was this what he was talking about? Was this the last secret?

Jessica moved toward Grandma. "If you attack one of us, you attack all of us."

Grandma released her collected energy. Jessica flew back, cracking the wall. Then she landed in a smoldering heap on the floor.

"No!" I shouted, envisioning lifting her by the throat. Grandma rose from the ground, hands clawing at her neck but finding nothing but her own skin. Fury and rage tightened their grip on me, and I felt myself slipping away, giving into my anger.

"Selene?" Katrina said, her eyes wide and a little scared.

"Check on Jess," I told her, not easing my grip on Grandma for a moment but managing to keep it from tightening.

"Selene, you're killing her," Leslie said, placing her hand on my arm. "This isn't you."

Good, a voice in my mind said. I was so startled I released everything. Grandma fell to the floor, gasping for air. "Put her in the chair."

Leslie went to her, and I could see her hands shaking as she helped Grandma up. I had almost crossed a line. Almost become what my grandmother was convinced I was. I looked over at Katrina and Jessica.

"She's breathing," Katrina said. "But we should probably take her to the hospital."

I nodded. "Take Grandma's car. Leslie can help you. My grandmother and I have a lot to talk about."

Neither of them said anything, though I felt their eyes on me. I used my will to keep Grandma immobile in her kitchen chair while they got out of the house. I sat down next to her and folded my hands. "Did you curse me?"

Her eyes met mine, but she didn't speak.

"Please. I'm asking for your help."

"I am helping you, child. I'm keeping you human."

"You're killing me."

She shook her head. "You're killing yourself." Her eyes met mine. "I told you to take the book and run. Not to let them find you, but you went with them. You went back to the Abyss, and now the evil you is coming through and tearing you in two."

"I'm not evil. Look at me. I am me. I have always been me. I swear to you I didn't kill my parents. I talked to Cheney about it. He said it wasn't my magic."

"'Whenever he tells a lie, he speaks in character, because he is a liar and the father of lies," she quoted the Bible at me.

I laughed. "You're a witch. Don't you think Bible quotes are a bit hypocritical?" Anger fought its way back to the surface. "After all, according to the Bible, I should suffer you to live." I rubbed on the sleeve of Cheney's shirt to remind myself to be calm.

She glared.

I crossed my arms over my chest and felt something in the shirt pocket. "Did you cast the curse? Do you know where Devin is?"

She looked away.

I rolled my eyes, sure she was guilty. I took the pouch the hoodoo priestess gave me off of my belt and laid it on the table. Grandma looked at it with a wary expression. "We can do this the easy way or the hard way." When she didn't respond, I said, "Fine. Hard it is."

I got a bowl and a knife and placed them on the table. I put the pouch in the bowl and mentally forced Grandma's hand over it. I ignored the fact that I felt nothing about what I was doing, and I raised an eyebrow at her.

Her glower didn't give me a moment's pause. I ran the knife over her palm and she hissed in pain. I watched the blood dribble into the bowl, keeping her arm suspended until the little sachet was soaked. Then I grabbed her injured hand and did as I had seen Cheney do before. I pushed my energy into her, making her heal faster. When the cut was no more than a faint pink line, I got up. A wave of dizziness washed over me and I gripped the table to steady myself, losing my magical hold on Grandma. I heard her push back from the kitchen table, and the next instant I was hit with a force that rivaled a freight train. I smashed against the brick wall, my head snapped back, and the lights went out.

TWENTY TWO

I awoke with a crushing pain in my skull and pressed my hand to my head. I forced my eyes open to look at the sticky red substance covering my hand. The room spun, and I retched to the side of my chair. I wasn't tied down though. After several deep, gasping breaths I stumbled toward the door, but I ran into an invisible wall. I looked at the floor. A circle had been painted beneath me. I felt for my phone before remembering I didn't have pockets and had left it at home. Shit.

"There's no way out," Grandma said.

"You have to let me go," I told her. "I'm trying to save a life."

"And I'm saving hundreds, maybe thousands."

"Call Cheney. Talk to him."

"He's blind to you. I have no doubt he's convinced himself that you didn't kill your parents, but I know the truth."

"Gah! I can't talk to you. *You* are killing three people tonight."

"The young witch was not my responsibility. She was yours. That death is on you. I have nothing against Cheney, but he should've known better than to bind himself to you."

I tried to use my power to throw her across the room, but it bounced back and hit me, knocking me into the invisible wall. I crumbled to the floor and stayed in a heap, struggling to think past the anger. There had to be a way out of here. As I was on the verge of giving up, it came to me. I took a deep breath and willed myself to transport, hoping she hadn't accounted for the fact that, despite her binding, I had managed to regain some of my elf abilities.

Unfortunately she had. "Damn it!" I yelled.

"Mind your tongue, Lene," she said, turning back to the sink with the bowl and my sachet in her hand.

Without a second thought, I released every ounce of energy I had. The entire house shuddered and shifted. Grandma clung to the counter and the foundation began to tremble. Her circle was powerful enough to prevent small attacks but it couldn't withstand the larger force. The windows exploded inward in a shower of glass shards and a three-inch wide crack zigzagged across the kitchen floor, slitting my magical prison in half.

Edith—I couldn't call her Grandma anymore—gasped when I appeared beside her. I snatched my blood-soaked sachet from the counter and walked away. "We'll talk again later," I said. Then I transported to the hospital.

The girls were still in the emergency room and Jessica was awake. They were huddled together, whispering when I walked in "You okay?" I asked Jess.

They all looked up at me. Leslie's hand shot up and covered her mouth.

"Selene," Katrina hissed, standing up and pushing me down into her seat. "You can't walk around looking like this."

"What?" I looked down at myself and saw what she meant. I was covered in blood and had the bloody bag clutched in my hand like a heart.

Katrina dug around in her purse until she found a plastic bag. I put the sachet into it, and she shoved it in her purse.

"Is she . . . you know?" Leslie said.

I shook my head and Leslie gasped. Maybe I didn't understand the question. "Is she *what*?" I asked, pressing my fingers to my temples, my head still throbbing.

"Your grandma. Is she okay?" she asked in a hushed tone.

I groaned. "She's fine. This is mostly my blood." I leaned forward until my head rested on my knees. A nurse rushed over to me and tried to get me to sit in a wheelchair. "No, no. We're not here for me. You need to check her."

"Selene, go with her," Jessica said. "I'm fine."

I shook my head. "No time."

"Don't make me call Cheney," Kat said.

Jessica gave Leslie a look and she stood up. "I'll come back with you."

Leslie and I headed back. I sat on the bed and waited for a doctor. "Seriously, I'll be okay. We have to go."

"You're bleeding all over and look terrible. Let them look at you." She perched her hands on her hips. "What happened?"

"We can't talk about it here."

The doctor walked in while Leslie was filling out the clipboard for me. "So what do we have here?" he asked.

"I fell and hit my head," I said, frowning at Leslie again for dragging me back here.

He asked me a ton of questions about how I fell and what I was feeling. I tried to answer them without getting impatient. "Well, let's take a look," he eventually said, coming closer.

His fingers parted the gooey mess of hair and parted it again in another spot. "Nasty gash," he muttered. "Did you lose consciousness?"

"No," I lied. There definitely wasn't time for CT scans.

An hour and a handful of stitches later we were finally leaving. We transported back to the castle. "I need to find wood from an ash tree and sage. I'll meet you guys in the garden," I told them and headed in the opposite direction, looking for a guard who might be able to help me. I asked the first couple I came across, but they had no idea where in the castle I could find what I was looking for. I stumbled up to my room, dizzy and weak. I didn't think I could transport anywhere. I found my phone and called Cheney, but he didn't answer. I dialed Sy and explained what I needed. He said he'd get it and meet me.

On the way back to the garden, I ran into Sebastian. "Where's Cheney?" I asked.

"What happened to you?" He took me by the arm, propping me up.

I sighed. "Edith happened. Where's Cheney?"

"Haven't seen him. I thought he was with you."

Everything in me stopped. "No. He was supposed to be with you today."

Sebastian nodded. "I know. We were on our way to meet with the Sehkmet bounty hunter and he said he changed his mind. He needed to help you with your grandmother. So I went on my own and he came to you."

I shook my head. "No, he didn't make it." Maybe he was working on the council business.

"Maybe you just missed one another," Sebastian said, concern coloring his face. "Honestly, Selene, you don't look good. I think you need to rest."

"No," I nearly shouted. "I have to break the curse."

"So your grandma did set it?"

"She wouldn't come out and admit it, but I know she did." I started walking again. "I have to finish this."

Sebastian helped me down to the garden where Sy and the girls waited—flirting and laughing. Sebastian mumbled something under his breath that had the distinct tone of jealousy. If it hadn't felt like my head had taken up residence in a nutcracker, I would've laughed.

"Selene," Sy said when he saw me. "What happened?" He rushed to my side.

"She got her ass handed to her by an old lady," Jessica said with a snicker.

I flipped her off and brushed the guys away. "Stop fussing. I look worse than I am." As the last word left my lips, another wave of nausea washed over me. I rushed to the bushes, heaving.

I wiped my mouth on Cheney's ruined shirt sleeve and went back to the group watching me like I might keel over any minute. "Let's do this."

Sy and Leslie made a campfire and dropped in the sage. Katrina pulled out the plastic bag and handed it to me. "Does anyone have a knife?" I asked.

Sebastian handed me a thin, wicked looking dagger. I sliced my palm and squeezed it over the opening of the bag. When the sachet was glistening again, I pulled it out and tossed it in the fire. It crackled, sizzled, and popped, making the flames turn different colors. Then, with a poof, the fire snuffed itself out.

"Is that it?" Sebastian asked.

"Were you supposed to say anything," Katrina asked.

"Nope, that's it," I said.

"Do you feel any different?" Sy asked.

I shook my head.

"Do you remember anything new?" Jessica tried.

I didn't. Everything was the same.

"Maybe it takes a while to kick in," Leslie said and I nodded, knowing that wasn't the case.

"It's not going to work, guys." Grandma hadn't cursed me. Someone else did and she knew who it was, but Toinette said I only had one chance. I slumped to the ground, tears streaming down my cheeks. I failed. I couldn't break the curse. I couldn't find Devin.

The girls surrounded me, telling me it would be fine. It would all work out. We just needed to find another away. I snapped. "Will you just leave me alone?" I bellowed. "It isn't going to be fine. Devin is dead. I'm probably next and with me goes Cheney. Hopefully I die before I go on some angry killing rampage and hurt all of you. Go home. You don't belong here."

I stood up and stalked toward the maze.

"Don't give up," Sy called after me.

I turned around and threw up my arms. "It's hopeless.

Now is the perfect time to give up. Take them home, Sy. Once I'm gone they'll be safe anyway."

I didn't make it far before Sy fell into step with me. "Go away."

"No." He put his arm over my shoulder. "We'll go back to that priestess and get another one of those pouch thingies."

"She said I only had one chance."

"Well, she's never known you. I've never seen one person get more chances in life than you, coz. This is a hurdle, not a mountain."

"Okay, let's say I do get another sachet. Then what?" I looked at him. "Edith won't tell me who cast the spell, and I have no hope of finding the person before the harvest moon."

"We'll make her talk."

I raised an eyebrow. "Are you seriously suggesting I torture my grandmother?"

He laughed. "Selene, there are more ways than one to make someone talk. You're friends with a jinn—an impressively powerful one."

"I don't think Holden's going to grant me any wishes."

"Holden has methods—nonviolent ones—for making people tell him their deepest, darkest secrets. And if that doesn't work, we can always send in Olivia. Don't underestimate either of them. They pack a one-two punch that the Abyss probably isn't ready for."

"And yet they couldn't find Michael or Devin."

He shrugged. "Finding someone and working someone who is already found are two completely different things. I'm just saying you have resources available to you. It would be absurd to give up now."

"Who's giving up?" Cheney's voice came from behind

us and my heart leapt.

I turned, already feeling stronger with him there. "No one."

He smiled. "I didn't think so."

I went to him and he wrapped his arms around me while I rested my head on his shoulder.

"You know, I never understood what the two of you possibly saw in one another."

"It's not the time, Sy," I said.

"But I think I understand why it works now," he continued, ignoring me. "You bring out the best in each other. She's less moody with you—"

Cheney laughed. "You mean she gets more moody when I'm not here? How did you survive her so long?"

"Years and years of practice." Sy winked at me. "And she makes you tolerable."

I shook my head. "Thank you for your analysis."

"Anytime. It's probably a good thing you aren't coming back to the bar—no room for you anyway."

I let go of Cheney and stood on my tiptoes to kiss Sy's cheek. "Thank you for everything."

"I'll get Baker to take us back tomorrow." He gave me a quick hug and disappeared.

"Looks like you need to catch me up again." Cheney led us to a bench where I told him all about Edith and our ruined chances of removing the curse.

Worry lines creased the edges of his mouth. "We'll get another sachet and your grandmother will talk. I don't care what lengths we have to go."

"She also said you came back that night when I was seven and told her I killed my parents."

He took my hands. "I absolutely did no such thing."

"Well, you're never going to convince her of that."

"But you believe me?"

I nodded. I did.

"My friends hate me now."

He chuckled softly, and goose bumps washed over my skin. "None of them left. They went back to their rooms. They understand." His hand went under my hair to the back of my neck and immediately I started feeling better. I pulled away. "No healing. It shortens your life."

"I'm not going to sit here with you in pain. It doesn't shorten it enough to matter." He tugged me back to him.

"Where were you today?"

"I checked your grandma's house, but you weren't there. Then I met with some council members."

"I tried to call you."

He nodded. "I didn't want to interrupt our meeting."

"I'm glad you're here now." I bit my lip to keep it from trembling.

"We'll stay together tomorrow. I promise."

TWENTY THREE

Cheney and I met Baker, Femi, Holden, and Olivia at the Office the next morning. Olivia smiled when we walked through the door holding hands and elbowed Holden. "I told you so."

He rolled his eyes. "That doesn't prove anything."

Cheney gave me a questioning look, but I didn't know what they were talking about either. "I told you not to rush into breaking the bond. I knew you could work things out," Olivia said, hugging me in greeting.

I smiled and was about to thank her when Cheney spoke. "Oh, we're still breaking the bond."

Olivia looked from me to him, her eyes worried, and Holden elbowed her, a slight smile twitching his lips.

"Let's get this show on the road." Femi boosted herself up to sit on the bar.

"Off that bar," Sy said before she even landed.

I watched with mild interest, but inside I was reeling. Cheney *wanted* to break the bond. He'd been acting so strange the last couple days, and pieces began to fall together. He was leaving me.

Femi slid back to her feet. "Okay, I think we have a lead

on your friend."

"Really?" All thought of my love life vanished. "Where?"

It surprised me when Olivia stepped forward. "I'm not sure where exactly, but I have it narrowed down. Wherever she is, she's surrounded by very strong magic. I can't quite hone in on her." Olivia's eyes rolled up and she rocked back slightly, tilting her head as if listening to something. Then she went back to normal and pulled a little sheet of paper out of her jeans pocket.

"These are the locations I think are most likely." She had at least twenty addresses listed. "Baker and Holden helped me track them down. They all have a strong natural magic, which would help mask her location."

"Have you gone to any of them?" Cheney asked.

"No. We just finished the list. I wanted to let Selene know we're working on it."

"Thank you," I said.

"Cheney can have elves check these locations," Sy said. "I think Selene needs your help with something else."

Everyone looked at me. "Well, I need help getting my grandmother, Edith, to tell me who cursed me."

Holden laughed. "Your grandma? What has happened to my life?"

"Of course we'll help," Olivia said.

"Great." I let out a breath. "And Baker, can you take us back to see Toinette?"

"I sure can, baby, but I wouldn't recommend it."

"They don't have a choice, Baker," Sy said.

He started to say something else, but Holden cut him off. "Just do it."

Baker rubbed his eyelid. "Fine. Don't say I didn't warn ya."

"Okay, cool. Thanks." I tried to swallow the nervousness bubbling up in my throat. "So Cheney and I will go with Baker to see Toinette, and Sy can work with Sebastian to organize the search for Devin. Once I have another sachet, I will call you, Olivia and Holden, to help with Edith."

Everyone nodded but Cheney. He pressed his lips together. "May I speak with you for a moment?"

I followed him off to the side. "What's wrong?"

He sighed. "We don't want to involve the elves in this."

"Why not?"

"Because we still don't know who took her or what they know. Your secret could be exposed." He gave me a meaningful look.

"But—"

"We'll find her. Why don't you go with Baker and Femi, and I'll call Sebastian, and those of us who can transport will start looking."

I nodded. "What if Toinette won't give me another sachet?"

He kissed my forehead. "You're very persuasive. I have every confidence you'll get it."

We told everyone the new plan. They agreed, and moments later Baker, Femi, and I were back in New Orleans, but unfortunately the laundromat was closed.

"You wouldn't happen to know where she lives, would you?" I asked, eyeing the dark storefront. We could probably break in pretty easily. All I needed was one personal item of hers.

"Don't look so worried, doll. We'll go door to door.

That's why we have dogs."

"What dogs?"

Baker laughed and started walking to the first house. "Feet," Femi clarified. "I personally think he talks like that because he likes to confuse people."

"You know, if we broke in and grabbed something of hers, this could go a lot faster."

Femi shrugged. "I have no problem with that plan. These boots were not made for walking." I looked down at her feet. Her black boots laced up the front and sported three-inch heels of some sort of metal that was amazingly silent when she walked. "They were actually made for ass-kicking, special order." She gave me a Cheshire grin. "Hey, Baker, hold up."

She jogged up to him and I hustled to keep up. "Why don't we break in and let Hermione do her thing."

"What's that, kitten?"

Femi bared her teeth. "That's one." She flicked up a sharpened fingernail.

"I can track her if I have something of hers," I explained.

Baker shook his head. "Not a chance. You trying to get me bumped off? First off, no one breaks in there who doesn't have a death wish. Second, if Toinette doesn't want to be found, you ain't gonna find her through magic. Third, there's no guarantee where any of the stuff in there came from or what it could lead you to."

"And you honestly think anyone around here is going to tell us anything?" I crossed my arms over my chest.

"Watch and learn."

Baker morphed into Toinette right before my eyes, even down to the clothing. He winked and sashayed up the porch steps before ringing the doorbell.

"Mama Toinette," the woman who answered the door said, looking a little frightened. "Do you want to come in?" Her voice was practically shaking.

"No, child." He even sounded like her. "I'm feeling a might dizzy. Would you mind walkin' me home?"

Her eyes grew to the size of beach balls. "To your home?"

Baker nodded.

"Umm, here, sit down." The woman offered the chair on the porch. "I'll get my jacket."

When she was gone, Baker looked back and grinned in a way that made Toinette's face appear sinister. I shuddered. "That's creepy, but amazing."

"Shape-shifters have it so easy," Femi said, rolling her eyes.

The woman walked Baker to a cemetery while Femi and I trailed behind a respectable distance away. By the time we made it to the cemetery gate, she was gone and Baker waited for us, looking normal.

"Wouldn't take me past the gates," he said. "She was tad jumpy."

"Toinette lives in a cemetery?" I asked.

He shrugged. "Maybe that's just what she wants people to think. Who knows?"

"Well, what are we waiting for?" Femi scaled the gate that was more than twice my height like it was nothing.

"She did that in heels," I said.

Baker laughed. "You want a boost?"

I gave him a look. "I don't climb fences." I focused on the lock until there was an audible click. Baker and I found

Femi lounging on top of a grave. "Will you get off that?" I hissed.

Femi looked around. "Why?"

"That is someone's grave."

"They're dead. I don't think they care." Femi hopped down. "Toinette," she bellowed, cupping her hands megaphone style around her mouth.

Baker leaned against the gate, watching with obvious amusement. Irritation flared in me. I needed Toinette to help me, not to be offended by the company I kept.

"Who's hollering? You'll wake the dead." Toinette came around a tombstone fifty feet away.

"Found her," Femi said.

I groaned and walked to meet the older woman. "I'm sorry about that—and even more sorry to bother you on your," I looked around, "day off." Her eyes weren't milky and blind as they were before. What was going on? "What happened to your eyes?" I asked before I could stop myself.

"Have you come to pay the price?"

"No. I used it on the wrong person. May I please have another gris gris bag?"

She looked at me until I squirmed. "I warned you not to waste it."

"I know. I thought I had the right person. Edith even attacked me, but it wasn't her. I did what you said and nothing happened."

She took my hands and shook her head gravely. "I cannot give you another. The cost is too great for you to bear."

"I don't care what the cost is," I said, and it was true. Even if it cost my life, at least I would be able to save Devin and Cheney before I went. "Please."

She looked up at the sky and muttered to herself. "Okay. But I will come for you. The spirits will have to be appeased. I don't know what they will require, but it will be no small task. If you do not uphold your end of the bargain..." She shook her head and rested her hand on a tombstone.

I bit my lip but forced a smile. "Thank you."

"Follow me." She led me up and down so many rows of graves that I had no idea how to get back. We finally stopped in front of an ancient, battered crypt with crumbling stonework. I shuddered when I saw a hole in the side of the structure that could only be a doorway to the inside of the tomb.

I steeled myself, ready to enter if that's what she demanded. She stooped down and picked up a chipped piece of the wall. "Give me your arm." She pressed the rock hard into my forearm and pulled it all the way down to my wrist. A paper-thin trail of blood was left in its wake. She then smashed the stone of the tomb and picked up the small piece that chipped off. She rolled it in the blood on my arm and placed it in a sack she had around her neck.

She led me around the cemetery, collecting a bizarre assortment of items. When she was pleased with the contents, she pulled the drawstring closed and pressed the bag to her lips, whispering in a language I didn't understand. The wind picked up, blowing my hair into my face. Gray clouds rolled in. I struggled to listen to her.

She pressed the sachet into my hand. "The same as before. A third gift is not possible."

I swallowed. "I understand. If all goes well, Cheney and I will be back tonight for you to break the bond. Is that okay?"

"Yes. Meet me here before 2:00 a.m.—not a moment later."

"Okay."

Her head jerked to the left, as if she'd heard something. "Go now. Quickly, before they can claim their price," she said, pushing me away.

I walked away, hoping I was going in the right direction. I felt eyes on me, but every time I turned around, nothing was there. I picked up my pace, ignoring the chill on my neck. I was nearly running by the time I made it to the main row. Baker and Femi were in sight, but whatever was behind me felt like it was breathing on my neck. I started to sprint. I didn't stop when I got to them, just continued right out the gate. As soon as both feet were on the other side of the boundary, everything quit. The wind stopped whipping around me. The sky was blue and cloudless again. I looked back as Baker and Femi made their way toward me. "What's the rush?" Femi asked. "Did you get what you came for?"

"I got it," I said weakly. I got it and maybe more than I'd bargained for.

TWENTY FOUR

We found Olivia and Holden standing together, laughing on the beach in front of Edith's house. Holden spotted us first.

"You want me to charm your grandmother?" His voice was the most animated I'd ever heard it.

"If you can." I rubbed a hand over my face. "She's powerful. Don't turn your back on her or let your guard—"

Holden held up his hand. "I got this."

I shook my head, wringing my hands as he ambled toward the now windowless house with foundation problems.

"Don't be nervous. Holden won't hurt her," Olivia said.

"I'm less worried about him hurting her than I am about her hurting him. Last time I talked to her, she gave me a concussion."

Olivia brushed a piece of hair out of her face. "Is it wrong that I sort of hope she gets the upper hand?" She laughed and I looked at her in shock. "He heals fast. He'll be fine. It will be too much fun to tease him about for the next hundred years or so. But if she does hurt him, we better get inside quick."

Olivia and I joined Baker and Femi, who were watching

the house, and I felt the relief of Cheney being near before I saw him.

"Sorry I'm late," he said, kissing me on the cheek.

A few minutes later, Holden came to the door and waved us inside.

"Whoa. You really did a number on the house this time, didn't you?" Cheney said as we walked up the steps.

I was about to answer when I remembered that he said he had come by Edith's house, but I wasn't there. If he came after I talked to her last time, he would've already seen it. I frowned. Maybe I was overthinking it, and even if I wasn't, this was the least of my concerns. "Yeah, I guess."

We all squeezed into the small living room. Holden sat between my grandmother and Olivia, scowling as Edith rubbed his leg. Baker leaned against the fireplace, and Femi and Cheney took the chairs while I paced.

"What is she doing here?" Edith asked when she finally noticed I was in the room.

"Selene has some questions. Could you answer them for her?" Holden said in a bored voice.

Her eyes narrowed, but she nodded.

"Did you curse me?"

"I helped. It was the least I could do."

"Who did you help?"

She pointed directly to Cheney. "Him."

Everyone went still.

"Shh," Holden said, touching her forehead. Edith lulled back on the couch, asleep.

Holden moved away from her and seemed to shake off whatever he'd been doing.

"Cheney?" I said.

He shook his head. "I have no idea what she's talking about. I didn't return that night. I wouldn't have risked exposing where you were."

But this was twice that she'd said he had been there, and this time I was pretty confident she was telling the truth. Cheney had been acting odd recently. He said he'd visited the house but acted like he hadn't seen it. He was withdrawn and removed.

"What are the chances she wasn't telling the truth?" Olivia asked Holden.

Holden shrugged. "It's like being drunk. You lose a lot of inhibitions, but if she's been lying to herself long enough to believe her own stories, anything's possible—including that she'd lie without knowing it."

"And *he* could be lying. He might've cursed her." Femi stepped in front of Cheney.

"It makes no sense for me to curse her when it would also harm me."

"True," Holden said.

My mind spun. Cheney may not have cursed me, but something was going on with him and I couldn't continue to ignore it.

"I think you guys are missing the obvious solution," Baker said.

I looked over at him, and he morphed into Cheney.

"Blah, blah, blah. Elf things," he said in Cheney's voice. Then he winked and returned to his usual stocky build and red hair. "It's easy enough to fool somebody."

"Yeah, if you're a shifter," Femi said.

"Bingo," Baker told her.

"Do you know any shifters?" I asked

He shook his head. "No."

"Not that you know of anyway," Baker said. "Anyone can be a shifter." Baker took my arm and pulled me into the kitchen. Then he morphed into me and walked into the living room while I stayed put.

"What's going on?" Cheney asked.

"Baker just wanted to tell me something," he said in my voice.

"And prove a point," I said, stepping out.

Cheney looked back and forth between us and whistled. "So you're saying it is impossible to find out who cursed her."

"I don't know if it's impossible, but it certainly isn't going to happen today," Baker said.

I closed my eyes. *Damn it.*

"Okay, well, we'll keep thinking about this, but let's finish looking for your friend," Olivia said with sympathetic eyes.

Everyone got up slowly, leaving Edith asleep on the couch, and headed out. Olivia pulled Cheney to the side and spoke to him in a hushed tone. Holden came over to me.

"Your grandmother should wake up in an hour or so."

"Okay," I said, but I was preoccupied watching Olivia whisper to Cheney. What was going on?

"I don't know if this matters to you or not, but she does care about you."

I finally looked at Holden. "Excuse me?"

"Your grandmother. She cares about you." He seemed so uncomfortable it made me uncomfortable.

"She has a funny way of showing it."

"She thinks she's losing you and it's making her hold on

tighter." He cleared his throat. "I just thought you might want to know."

With that, he walked over and joined Olivia. Cheney came to me. "What was that all about?" I asked.

"Nothing. We were just talking about the list. I'm going to go back to the castle with you."

"Why aren't we helping?" I needed some sort of win today. I wasn't going to let everything slip away without a fight.

"They have it covered. Let's just go back."

"Are you giving up?" My heart was breaking.

"Come back with me, please."

"I don't want to give up."

"What else can we do?" His eyes lit and turned hot. "I'm tired. I'm tired of fighting and surprises. I'm sorry you're cursed, but you brought it on yourself, and now you're taking me down with you."

He walked a few steps before turning around. "But that's my own fault. Everyone warned me about you."

I closed my eyes. "I'll go to the Office." I fought the lump in my throat.

"Typical. Running away as soon as I express anything negative about you. But guess what, you're not perfect."

"I know I'm not perfect." My voice shook, but I couldn't stop it. "I know I messed up and I'm sorry. Maybe I can't fix this, but that doesn't mean I am going to stop trying. Help me." I took his hand. "I'm sorry I ruined your life."

He yanked his hand away. "You really want to fix it, break the curse."

"I can't."

"You haven't even tried. Why the hell did you become a

changeling? You're supposed to have all kinds of power, but you can't do anything. I don't want to die. I have a kingdom to run. I have plans. Break the damn curse."

"I can't," I whispered.

He glared at me. "How about this? I kill one of your friends every hour until you get off your ass and break the fucking curse yourself. You're a witch and an elf. There is no way a little hoodoo should take you out."

"I know you won't hurt my friends."

A slow smile spread over his lips. "Won't I?"

He disappeared and I stood in shock. What had gotten into him? Worry trickled in. He wouldn't hurt my friends, would he? I transported to the castle and ran frantically from room to room, looking for them. I found Cheney with Jessica, Katrina, and Leslie lined up in his office.

"What's going on?" Leslie asked, her voice quivering.

I ignored them and focused on him. "You're scaring them. Stop it."

"You stop it." He pulled out a knife. "Do I need to prove my resolve?"

I rolled my eyes. "He's not going to hurt you," I told them. "You're not going to hurt anyone—"

He hurled the knife. It hit Jessica with a thump. She made a noise and fell to the floor. Katrina or Leslie, maybe both of them, screamed, but it barely registered. White-hot fury rushed through my veins and roared in my ears. I lunged for Cheney, clawing at his throat. "I'll kill you," I snarled.

He laughed, infuriating me further. "You'll only kill yourself," he said, escaping my hold.

Cheney drew a sword from thin air. I glanced around, but I had no weapons. The tip of his sword came so fast I couldn't get out of the way in time, and it slashed my left arm. I growled and he lunged again. A sword appeared in my hand, and I blocked him with such force he stumbled back. He smiled wide and dropped his sword, but I wasn't done with him. Cheney had been a pain in the ass since the first day I met him. Always fighting with me, always getting under my skin.

I lifted him by the throat with my mind. I became a changeling to save this jackass and now he was killing my friends. He was no better than Jaron. Those endless conversations about how our rebellion was about the king and how Cheney would never get hurt, only to hear him talking about how he was going to kill both of them and take the throne himself. He had lied to me, lied to me for years, but even he never attacked my best friends. I squeezed Cheney's throat tighter.

"Selene, let him go," Katrina said.

I ignored her.

"Shit, Selene, I'm bleeding over here. Let him go." Jessica's voice came from the floor, startling me.

I looked back at them.

Leslie shrugged. "Plan B."

I released my hold on Cheney immediately. He fell to the floor, coughing and rubbing his throat. "It was Olivia's idea. She could feel the power in you. I just had to get you to release it—but the only way I knew how to get you to act without thinking was to make you mad or scare you."

"So you stabbed my friend."

He gave me a half smile. "I have excellent aim." He went over and helped Jessica up, pulled out the knife, and healed the wound.

"So is that it? Is the curse broken?" Jessica asked.

I remembered. I remembered everything. "I never gave Jaron my memories," I said and sank into a chair, letting that night, the night my human parents, Jim and Laurel, died, replay in my mind. I didn't know who or what killed them, but Cheney was right—it wasn't me. I'd been out walking in the woods, thinking about the two men I left behind to become *this*. I hated being a child. It was degrading. But I had to perpetuate the illusion. I looked ruefully at the stuffed rabbit clutched in my tiny hand. Ridiculous. When I got home, dinner aromas—garlic and basil and fresh yeasty bread were thick in the air. Something felt off though. I wandered to the kitchen. A pot of water was boiling over, and a frying pan of tomato sauce was popping and spattering the stove. I stood on my tiptoes and flicked everything off, a bad feeling nesting in my stomach. I dropped the stuffed animal, Peter, to the floor and went to look for them. I found their bodies in the hallway, as if they'd been running away. They'd been mauled, but there were no signs or scent of animal—no sensory clues about the attacker of any kind—in the house. It wasn't natural. My control slipped and I screamed. Old anger and resentment rushed back, and I ceased to see anything until Cheney appeared in front of me.

That was the night I met Edith, but I didn't want to go with her. I didn't want to attach to another human, not when they couldn't defend themselves against the fae, and I knew what happened to Jim and Laurel had everything to do with me. At Edith's house I went to bed, still in shock, and the next morning I didn't remember anything. I was just like any other human child.

But that didn't explain how Jaron was able to give me

memories real enough to fool me—though most of them were fabricated. I never intended to physically harm Cheney. I was maneuvering him to be an ally against his father, and that worked. But what was Jaron maneuvering me toward? "He's manipulating me."

"It doesn't matter now. You broke the curse." Katrina pulled me up. "Everything's going to be okay." She hugged me, and Jessica and Leslie joined in. I was going to live. Cheney was going to live. Jessica was okay. We would get Devin back. Grandma cared about me.

I broke away from them. "I need to sit down." I felt a little dizzy.

"You okay?" Cheney asked.

The things he'd said still echoed in my mind. I understood he was trying to make me mad, but they had roots. I had done too much, messed up too many times. "I'm fine."

"We'll give you guys some space," Leslie said, pulling the others out of the room. Cheney and I looked at each other.

"I don't know how you did it."

"Did what?"

"Pulled the knife. Only royalty has a holding."

I shrugged.

"Maybe it's a power thing," he said more to himself than to me. "So you remember everything?"

"I do." I didn't feel any differently about him now than I did before, but I wasn't positive he still felt the same way.

Cheney looked at the floor. "Then I guess we can break the bond."

The air burned in my lungs. "Yeah, I've already arranged it."

"I'm ready when you are."

My heart screamed for me to tell him I'd changed my mind. I didn't want to do it anymore. I wanted to stay bonded with him, even if it complicated things. I wanted to make it work. Yet my brain kept me quiet. There was too much between us and I had betrayed him one too many times. I didn't deserve any more chances and I knew it. I couldn't keep making selfish decisions. If Cheney wanted out, I wouldn't stop him.

TWENTY FIVE

The sun had set and the cemetery was dark. Cheney followed me inside and caught my arm before I turned down the first row.

"Selene, I just want you to know—"

"Have you broken the curse?" Toinette said, appearing out of nowhere.

I tore my eyes away from Cheney. "We did. And I didn't use the gris gris bag. Do you want it back?" I held it out to her.

"Once a gift is given, it cannot be taken back. Follow me." She led us into the mausoleum and instructed that we face each other. "Are you both sure you wish to break the bond?"

"Yes," Cheney said immediately.

"Of course," I said.

She bound our hands together with a scented leather rope and waved incense around us until I started to feel lightheaded. She dumped a pile of bones between us and chanted, moving in a slow counterclockwise circle. I felt Cheney's eyes boring into me, but I couldn't bring myself to look at him. She poured a clear alcohol on the ground surrounding us and set it on fire.

"Now pull the strap. Break free from it."

My eyes finally met his. He nodded and began to pull. I resisted, going in the opposite direction, so much like our lives. My muscles strained and shook as I fought not to allow myself to be pulled to him. The cord broke with a snap that sent a pulse outward. The fire burned away. I looked at Cheney. I didn't love him any less. I loved him exactly the same and my heart broke because I had ruined everything.

"It's done," I said.

"What do we owe you?" Cheney asked, his eyes wide and somewhat shell-shocked.

"Selene and I will settle accounts when the time is right," Toinette said.

"Is that all we need to do?"

She nodded, and I transported away as fast as I could. I went to the Office and was surprised to see it was open and that Sy was working. "I thought you were looking for Devin."

"Yeah," was all he said.

Why was everyone being so strange? I went back to his apartment and lay on the couch. I didn't have a yoga studio or income anymore. Maybe Sy would want a roommate. Chicago seemed like a nice town. I wouldn't mind bartending.

"What are you doing?" Cheney said from the doorway.

"Lying here."

"Why did you leave?"

"You meant the things you said earlier when you were trying to make me mad."

He nodded. "They're all true."

"Well then, problem solved. You're free and clear. I'll come back here. No harm, no foul."

"Don't be dumb, Selene. Yes, I meant every word I said—but I still love you. That has not, and will never, change. I want you in the castle. I chose you to be my wife and I still want that. You belong there. You will be a great ruler, once you're a bit less dramatic." He gave me a lopsided smile. "I can't always be here to pick you back up. You need to value yourself more for what's in here," he tapped my chest, "than for how other people see you."

"So you want me to come back?"

"Of course."

I laughed and wiped a tear away. "I'll get my stuff."

Cheney smiled, but his eyes had a flash of sadness. He kissed me softly. "I'll see you at home."

I found my last shoe under the couch and shoved it in my bag. When I straightened, Jaron stood in the doorway watching me.

"Going somewhere?" he asked.

A myriad of feelings stirred inside me. I had loved him for such a long time. I felt betrayed when I'd left, but now I'd had time to think about it. Something terrible made Jaron angry long before he met me. He hated the elves more than I ever could, but though I sympathized, I wasn't going to let his feelings sway me anymore. I said I wanted change, and Cheney and I could accomplish that together. Cheney made me happy; Jaron made me crazy.

"I'm going back to Cheney."

He swayed back as if I had hit him.

"Jaron, whatever happened, you need to let it go. Hatred has monopolized so much of your life. Fight it. Make a life for yourself. The Abyss is changing. We got what we wanted."

"So long as the Erlking still breathes the same air as me, I have not gotten what I wanted." His clipped words dripped bitterness. "How can you go to them?"

"It's not my fight anymore. Cheney has shown me what it is to love someone else—and that isn't what we had."

"This isn't over." Jaron's hands balled into fists, and his gray eyes were furious.

I walked toward him and the door. "I'm sorry, but it is. I won't let you hurt them anymore."

"Don't stand in my way, Selene. You can't stop this— the wheels are in motion."

"It's time for the fighting to end. Don't make me fight you. Just walk away." I brushed past him. I was waiting for Sy to finish making drinks and to come talk to me when my phone rang.

"Hello?"

"We found her," Sy's voice said from the other end of the line. I stared at him behind the bar, obviously not talking on the phone.

"Sy, how are you in two places?"

There was a pause. "Where are you?"

"At the Office."

"Ah." There was another pause. "Did you hear what I said? We found her. We found Devin."

I nearly dropped the phone. "Is she okay?" I asked when

Jaron walked out and broke my gaze from fake Sy for just a moment.

"Groggy, but unharmed. She was under some sort of sleeping spell and doesn't seem to know what happened."

"Did you find who took her?"

"No."

I shook my head, but I didn't care. We had Devin back and my memories. We could handle any challenge the world could muster up—unless . . . A faint trickle of worry seeped in. "Are you sure it's her?"

"What?" he asked with half a laugh.

"Edith thought Cheney came to see her, but he never did. I'm standing here staring at you and talking to a different you on the phone. Are you sure the Devin you have is my friend and not an impostor?"

He was quiet for a moment. "How can I tell?"

"Ask her what math class we met in."

I heard muffled talking before he came back. "She said it wasn't math. It was a history of witchcraft class and she asked for your notes."

I smiled. "It's her. Now, if this person behind the bar can be trusted, I'll meet you at the castle."

"You can always trust me." I heard the smile in Sy's voice. The other Sy walked down to where I stood.

"What do you need, Selene?"

I covered the receiver. "Do you know that I'm talking to you on the phone?"

He looked unconcerned. "Can I get you a drink?"

That was enough for me. I shook my head and went for the door. "Someday you're going to explain Sy 2.0 to me, coz."

Sy laughed. "Don't count on it. I'll see you soon."

Back at the castle, I went to the girls first and let them know Devin was on her way. Seconds later, Devin walked in with Femi, Baker, Sebastian, and Sy. Ear-piercing squeals and talking filled the room. I didn't stand back this time. I was in the thick of it. Even if they were human and would leave me, I was lucky to have them. I snuck out of the celebration and went to look for Cheney. He wasn't in any of the usual places. I checked our bedroom. No luck. I called him and heard his phone ringing in the closet. I followed the sound and found it lying on the floor next to the bloody shirt I'd worn the day before. I picked up the garment and slipped his phone in my pocket. It must've fallen out of his pants when he changed and he didn't notice. I carried the shirt to the bathroom and wadded it up to throw it away when I felt something in the pocket again. I pulled out a folded piece of paper that looked familiar.

I unfolded it with shaky hands.

One who has never sacrificed must learn that everything comes with a cost. Selene or you. The choice is yours. The human will go free if one of you comes to the ruins on the harvest moon.

Cheney said he had received a note but was vague about what it said. He had been acting secretive. He waited to wake up with me. He scrambled to finish setting up his council. Everything clicked together, right down to why, after never wanting to, he'd be so anxious to sever our bond. He had made sure that should he die, I would not. Cheney had been settling his affairs, saying goodbye.

TWENTY SIX

I heard voices as I went into the ruins. Two Cheneys faced off with one another. They were dressed identically and held themselves in the same stance. Without the bond pulling me, I couldn't tell which one was real and which was fake. They looked at me at the same time. I looked back and forth between them as I walked toward the front. No one spoke. Magic collected under my skin as my nerves frayed.

"I can't believe you came here without telling me," I said to whichever Cheney was the real one. "We agreed. No more secrets."

"Stay back," Cheney 1, who was standing to my right, said.

"You shouldn't be here," Cheney 2 said.

"No." I shook my head, still looking for any indication of who was who. "We said we were in this together. Bond or no bond, I'm staying."

Cheney 2 pulled a sword out of the air and lunged toward 1—who retrieved what looked like the exact same sword just in time to block. Metal clanged and sparked in a blur of motion as each met the other's defenses. They matched each other blow for blow, and I cringed each time one of them got close to the other. Cheney 1's sword clattered to the ground. 2 pulled back his blade for the final blow.

"No," I said, leaping between the two of them.

"Move," 2 growled.

I shook my head. "No. You'll have to kill me."

The sword wavered. "You're protecting the wrong one."

"I don't know that."

1 was back to his feet, sword once again in hand. He tried to move me out of the way.

I stomped my foot, releasing some energy, making the ruins tremble. "Hasn't there been enough bloodshed? Devin's dead. I'm not losing anyone else," I lied, watching both of their faces. 1's eyes washed with sadness. 2 looked momentarily confused. I hit him with the full strength of the energy I collected, but it never reached him. My attack reflected back and crashed over me, smashing me into the stone altar.

"Selene," the real Cheney said, coming to me.

The wind was knocked out of me, but I gestured and flailed as Jaron stepped forward.

"I knew you'd come. Unlike him, I never underestimate you. What gave me away?"

Cheney stood between us, sword in hand. "Who are you?" he asked.

I pushed up to my feet, my body protesting the movement. "Jaron, don't." I stepped around Cheney.

"I told you not to get in my way, Selene. I have waited too long. Only one of us will walk away tonight."

"You're Jaron," Cheney said. "Step aside, Selene."

"No." I didn't want anyone to get hurt. "Why do you hate him so much? Cheney has never hurt you."

Jaron glared at me. "Well, he has taken you."

I shook my head. "You hated him before that."

Jaron knocked me to the side. "He has my life. The life I was born to."

The fight started again, and thoughts swirled in my mind. Jaron had pulled a sword out of nowhere, and it wasn't the first time he'd done it. He had a holding and only royalty were supposed to have one. Who was he?

"What do you mean you were born to it?" I shouted above the sound of the fight.

"Haven't you figured it out yet? Don't you know where we are? This is where my father murdered my half-sister because she chose her human lover." Jaron resumed fighting with renewed strength and fury. He was bigger than Cheney, but Cheney was faster. Jaron had never told me anything about his past, and I'd never noticed. I was always happy to talk about mine, and he was a good listener. Cheney used Jaron's strength against him as he came charging at him, leaving Jaron off balance.

"That isn't possible," Cheney said as Jaron fell to the floor. "The only people who died here are—" His voice cut off and he stepped back. "You can't be."

"Yet here I am."

Cheney shook his head. "My father didn't—"

"Yes, that was your father's opinion on the matter as well, when he left me for dead as a baby. He wouldn't have his line disgraced with a half-elf," Jaron spat.

"He has a holding," I told Cheney and he nodded. "How are you a shifter?" I asked Jaron.

"I never said my mother was human." Jaron's eyes burned with hatred. "This was my life you were living. I have watched you get everything you want, never having to compromise or work. I am older. The kingdom should be mine by rights."

Cheney shook his head, looking stunned. "I didn't know."

"Like it would have made a difference. I have been in and out of your castle. I know what you are. I know what all of your kind are. Selene knows too, but somehow you managed to undo what I spent so many years building in her. I tried to bind her, bring her back to me. She was the one thing that was mine that you couldn't have, but you managed to steal her, too."

"You took my memories?"

"You betrayed me." Jaron's eyes softened slightly. "We had a good run. I thought we would end up together. I did love you, Selene. If only you stuck to the plan. . . ."

"If you wanted me dead that bad, why didn't you just kill me? Why send her to me?" Cheney asked.

"I wanted you to feel pain and betrayal like I felt. Only Selene was capable of doing that. I knew from the moment you pursued her. She was the only thing you ever worked at getting."

Cheney dropped his arm to his side. "I'm sorry for what my family has done. It was wrong. Give us a chance to set things right again."

"It's too late," Jaron said.

Cheney reached for me, but Jaron appeared behind me, pressing a knife to my throat. The cold metal bit into my skin and a warm tickle of blood ran down my neck. I held my breath, afraid that, if I moved, I'd be dead. "We had a deal. I let the human go. I am not responsible if she died after that.

My life was stolen from me. Either you give me yours, or I take it piece by piece, starting with Selene."

"Don't do it, Cheney," I said. "Let me go."

"I came here, didn't I?" Cheney said, ignoring me. He dropped his sword to the ground and held his arms out wide.

The knife eased away from my neck. Cheney's eyes met mine with an apology in them. Jaron flung the knife and it landed in Cheney's chest. He stumbled back, his hands clutching it as he dropped to his knees. His eyes never strayed from mine as he fell.

I didn't even try to break free from Jaron's grip, turning in his arms instead, hitting and scratching his face. "No!"

Jaron caught my arms and I crumpled to the ground. No. Cheney couldn't be dead. I couldn't breathe. Jaron released me and took half a step back.

"The problem, Selene, is that you know who I am, and now I can't take Cheney's place. You will never forgive me for Cheney, Michael, or your parents. I only wanted what should have been mine. You used to understand that. You and I, we used to be the same."

I shook my head. "I was never like you. You tried to make me like you." I stared at the floor, letting his words feed the pain inside of me like gasoline. I had only one chance. I would either die or save Cheney. I lunged for Jaron again, releasing all the energy I had built into the ground—and called a knife to my hand like I did before. The room shook and cracked. Jaron looked at the ground, and I rammed the blade into his heart all the way to the hilt. Blood poured over my fingers and his hand grabbed mine. I twisted the knife. Those gray eyes that used to look at me in love met mine, and hurt and betrayal crossed them. My body shook with adrenaline, and the light in Jaron's eyes went black. He fell to the ground and I watched him slowly evaporate as if he'd never been there at all. The ruins began to disintegrate and fall. I went back to Cheney and knelt beside him.

"Selene," he said weakly. He took my hand and squeezed. "I love you."

"I'm sorry," I whispered as walls fell. I pulled the knife out of his chest and pressed my hand over the wound. Blood pumped between my fingers. I pushed at the flow with my mind. It had to work. It had to. I would never survive without him.

EPILOGUE

It was all over. I couldn't believe I was still walking around, breathing, eating, *living* after everything I'd been through. I had nightmares that wouldn't stop. Taking Jaron's life wasn't something I would get over quickly or ever. I could justify my actions, yes—but logic didn't change my *feelings* about what I'd done. Worse than the images of Jaron, however, were those of Cheney—pale, beloved Cheney, bleeding out. . . . A pair of shoes entered my line of sight, making me look up. "Thank you for coming," I said, swiping at my tears and hugging Sy tight.

"I wouldn't miss it," he said. "Why are you crying? What did I tell you about elves and crying."

I gave a helpless gesture and laughed. "I don't know. I've been so emotional lately. Being human made me soft." I gave his cheek a peck.

I heard the door click behind me and a hand touched my lower back. "It's been an emotional couple weeks." Cheney kissed my temple. I still couldn't believe I'd been able to heal him. My energy had been zapped for days afterward, but it was worth it. We were together and stronger than ever.

"The two of you look happy," Sy said, his eyes sparkling.

"We are," I said.

"With Sy's arrival, the entire council is here now." Cheney smiled. "Are you ready, princess?"

"As ready as I'll ever be." The three of us were about to walk into the first official meeting when Baker came up.

"It's time, Selene," he said.

Cheney tightened his hand around mine. "Time for what?"

"To pay the spirits for their gifts. Toinette is requesting an audience." Baker's face was serious—and for once, there wasn't a trace of humor or joking in his voice.

I shivered. "But the meeting is about to start. Can it wait?"

He shook his head. "They choose the time. Making them wait could be bad."

I straightened my shoulders and kissed Cheney. "I'm sorry I have to miss out. I'll be home soon, and I want to hear all about it."

He set his jaw but nodded. I had to go. A deal was a deal. I wasn't scared. No matter what the spirits asked for, no matter what challenge they laid before me, I would make it through. I had my memory. I had my friends. I had my family. But most importantly, I had Cheney.

THE END

COMING SUMMER 2013

Book 3 in the Easy Bake Coven Series

Pickup Styx

Liz Schulte

ACKNOWLEDGMENTS

As always, I have to start with thanking my family and especially my mom for pushing me toward writing and publishing.

Producing a book takes a village. I am extremely lucky to work with such an amazing group of people. Without all of these people I don't know where I would be.

Ev Bishop — editing
Michelle Kampmeier — proofreading
Julie Titus — formatting
Once Upon A Time Covers — cover art
Promotional Book Tours and Mandie Stevens — promotions

And the best beta readers, friends, and writers in the world: Amanda Long, Tawdra Kandle, Olivia Hardin, C.G. Powell, Mandie Stevens, and Melissa Lummis.

Finally, my thanks have to go to the best and most amazing fans in the world. You guys keep me going and make me look forward to each and every day.

ABOUT THE AUTHOR

Many authors claim to have known their calling from a young age. Liz Schulte, however, didn't always want to be an author. In fact, she had no clue. Liz wanted to be a veterinarian, then she wanted to be a lawyer, then she wanted to be a criminal profiler. In a valiant effort to keep from becoming Walter Mitty, Liz put pen to paper and began writing her first novel. It was at that moment she realized this is what she was meant to do. As a scribe she could be all of those things and so much more.

When Liz isn't writing or on social networks she is inflicting movie quotes and trivia on people, reading, traveling, and hanging out with friends and family. Liz is a Midwest girl through and through, though she would be perfectly happy never having to shovel her driveway again. She has a love for all things spooky, supernatural, and snarky. Her favorite authors range from Edgar Allen Poe to Joseph Heller to Jane Austen to Jim Butcher and everything in between.

Books by Liz Schulte:

Secrets (Guardian Series Book 1)
Choices (Guardian Series Book 2)
Consequences (Guardian Series Book 3)

Dark Corners (Ella Reynolds Series Book 1)
Dark Passing (Ella Reynolds Series Book 2)

Easy Bake Coven (Easy Bake Coven Series Book 1)
Hungry, Hungry, Hoodoo (Easy Bake Coven Series Book 2)
Pickup Styx (Easy Bake Coven Series Book 3) – Coming Summer 2013

Dead Inside – Coming 2013
Frost's Kiss – Coming 2013
The Ninth Floor – Coming 2013

Anthologies

Cupid Painted Blind
Once Upon a Midnight Dreary

Learn more about Liz and her books at
www.lizshulte.com